Wild Cat

Wild Cat

by Jacques Poulin

Translated by Sheila Fischman

A CORMORANT BOOK

ONTARIO ARTS COUNCIL
CONSEIL DES ARTS DE L'ONTARIO

The publisher gratefully acknowledges the support of the
Canada Council for the Arts and the Ontario Arts Council
for its publishing program. We acknowledge the financial support
of the Government of Canada through the Book Publishing
Industry Development Program (BPIDP) for our publishing activities.

Printed and bound in Canada
First published in French as Chat sauvage by Leméac Éditeur Inc., Montreal

National Library of Canada Cataloguing in Publication Data

Poulin, Jacques, 1937–
[Chat sauvage. English]
Wild cat: a novel / Jacques Poulin; translated by Sheila Fischman.

Translation of: Chat sauvage.
ISBN 1-896951-50-3

I. Fischman, Sheila II. Title.

PS8531.082C4813 2003   C843'.54   C2002-905081-2
PQ3919.2.P664313 2003

Editor: Marc Côté
Cover and text design: Tannice Goddard
Cover image: Shelly Gifford
Printer: Friesens, Altona, Manitoba

Cormorant Books Inc.
62 Rose Avenue, Toronto, Ontario, Canada M4X 1N9
www.cormorantbooks.com

Wild Cat

Where does beauty go when it's erased,
Where do our thoughts go, and the dead
Pleasures of the flesh?
Cat, look away;
I see too much darkness in your eyes.

— CHARLES BROS, *THE SANDALWOOD BOX*

1

A Strange Visitor

My most distant ancestor sits in a glass cage in the Louvre Museum, in the Egyptian Antiquities section, and visitors walk around him, intrigued by the strange gentleness that has been lighting up his face for a period of four thousand years.

Everyone calls him "The Crouching Scribe." Wearing only a loincloth, he holds a papyrus on his knees and looks at his master with infinite patience as he gets ready to write down the words that will drop from the man's mouth.

That gentleness and patience were what led me to choose him as my model. There's a photo of him on the wall that faces my desk and I look at it often in the course of the day. That's what I was doing around six o'clock one evening, just before I closed my office, when all at once I heard the gate creak, then footsteps on the stairs and the sound of a chair in the waiting room.

Surprised at this visit so late in the day, I went down the corridor and opened the door. On the last chair sat an old man with white hair and bushy eyebrows. He held on his lap a grey raincoat and a battered hat. The cigarette in the corner of his mouth was out. He seemed lost in thought and didn't even turn his head in my direction. I realized that this was no ordinary client.

"Come in," I said.

He looked at me briefly and went into my office where he sat down without saying a word. I took from the drawer a pad of letter-paper and my old Waterman pen.

"What can I do for you?"

"I noticed your shingle when I was going by," he said after a brief hesitation. Then he fell silent. Under his thick white eyebrows his eyes, set very deep, were half-closed as he stared at me.

I tried to hold his gaze. Though I've been plying my trade for many years, clients still make an impression on me, often they make my heart beat faster, and I don't dare look at them directly right away.

"And?"

"You're so young," he said.

His remark made me smile; I was fifty years old, after all.

"Youth isn't a disability, you know!"

I was counting on that stale joke to lighten the atmosphere, but it was not a success. On the contrary, for a fraction of a second I thought I could see a strange glimmer in the old man's eyes. I got out of my swivel chair and went to the window and as if we had all eternity before us, I took the time to study the garden with the hedge of honeysuckle turning green, the Japanese cherry tree and the bare-branched birch, the white metal table and chairs. Pretty Cat was sleeping on the doorstep of the shed.

The cat noticed me and she had a long stretch in the slanting sunlight. I stretched a little too. Then, without turning around and as neutrally as possible, I asked: "Do you want to write to someone?"

"Yes," he said. "To my wife."

Usually people come to see me for a curriculum vitae or for official letters that require a particular vocabulary and phrases. But others come for love letters: they are always hesitant, they seem to have secrets or old wounds and it's most important not to rush them.

I went back to my chair.

"Your wife?" I repeated softly.

"That's right," he said.

"Has she . . . gone away?"

"Yes."

I uncapped my pen and bent over my writing pad to let the old man know that I was waiting for the rest, but he withdrew once more into his silence. Then from upstairs came the sound of saucepans: my friend Kim was starting to fix supper and she was probably wondering what was keeping me from going up to her place.

Without showing a hint of impatience, I asked: "Have you got her address?"

"Naturally, if I want to write to her!"

"Sorry . . ."

He had raised his voice and now was looking at me suspiciously. I assumed a confused look and gave up on the wife's address; it wasn't indispensable. What I did need to know though was why she had left, her current situation, her character, her feelings, and the feelings of the old man. The usual, in a word.

I began with a general question: "Would you like to tell me a little about your wife?"

It was at this very moment that Pretty Cat, who had climbed up the birch tree and crept to the end of a branch, jumped onto the windowsill and began to meow, pressing herself against the glass. I went over to open the window.

"On second thought," said the old man as he got up, "I'll come back another time."

"Are you sure?" I asked.

"Yes."

"Very well, I'll give you an appointment."

"That's not necessary."

He donned his raincoat, which was of military cut, with wide lapels, shoulder straps, and a belt that he tied with a knot and then, holding his hat, he left without saying goodbye. I heard him go down the stairs.

Pretty Cat rubbed up against my legs.

"See what you did?" I asked.

She purred. She was a young cat, black with white spots, and very intelligent. She always guessed when it was mealtime and she knew how to persuade me to go up to Kim's. I picked her up and when I walked out of the office I had the impression as usual that the Scribe was watching me.

2

Kim

No sooner had I started up to Kim's place than I saw her leave her apartment and go down the first steps. She was wearing one of the famous blue silk kimonos that were responsible for her nickname. Every time she bent her knee on her way down a step, the flash of light from her garment was a feast for the eyes.

With oven mitts on, she was carefully holding a Pyrex casserole that was giving off a delicious aroma that I knew very well.

"I made a shepherd's pie!" she declared.

"I know that smell!" I said.

Inside my place, she set the casserole on a hot pad in the middle of the table and the aroma filled the kitchen. Then she put her arms around me, patted my back with her heavy mitts, and hugged me very tight. Her soft, generous curves spread over my chest, wiping out the fatigue of the day. Unmoving, my eyes shut, I was making the pleasure last, but she loosened her arms.

"Did your work go well today?" she asked.

"Fairly well."

I couldn't ask her the same question, because we had different schedules. She was a kind of therapist, looking after people who were having trouble with life, and often it was in the evening — and sometimes even at night — that her clients needed her services. Though she'd been trained as a Jungian, she used a personal method of treatment, which relied as much on physical as on psychological means. When patients came during the night, they were asked to use the fire escape that went up from the garden to her apartment on the second floor in order to create as little disturbance as possible.

She dished up a big helping of shepherd's pie for me, and a more modest one for herself, and an even smaller one for the cat. who had already polished off her kibble. To make it cool off more quickly, I divided mine into four sections and poured some Heinz ketchup between them.

"This is really good!" I said, swallowing a small mouthful.

"Thank you," she said. "Were you working late?"

"Yes. I had a weird visit. Up till then it had been a very ordinary day: three CVs, an application for a civil service job, some editing for the Laval alumni publication, and in my spare time a little translation . . ."

"Routine, in other words."

"And then this strange old man showed up . . ."

"Strange in what way?"

To satisfy our curiosity, but also for mutual support, we were in the habit of telling each other about our day. I described the Old Man, his hesitations and the disconcerting look in his eyes. Then, to make it more interesting, I began to invent all sorts of details until my visitor became a mysterious character whose gloomy soul held secrets that could turn my life upside down.

Kim's eyes were shining like neon lights and a little glimmer warned me that her mother hen's instincts had been roused. She was afraid I was going to get into trouble. She'd stopped eating and Pretty Cat hopped onto the table and started to clean off her plate. My heart sped up, but five seconds later it was back to normal: that happened often since the operation.

While she waited till it was time to go back up to her place, Kim lay down with me on my leather sofa, which you sank into as if it were an inflatable dinghy that hadn't been blown up properly. She had me lie on my side with my knees bent and my back to her, and she lay behind me. Pretty Cat joined us and nestled against my stomach. Kim arranged her knees behind mine, wrapped her arms around me and slipped her warm hands inside my sweater; the cat started to purr very loudly, letting her know that we couldn't be in a better position.

When she left me I didn't even know: I was asleep.

3

Lights in the Night

Half asleep, I heard the footsteps of a patient going up the fire escape. A small hint of jealousy pinched at my heart and finished the job of waking me. It was a petty feeling, but I couldn't stop myself from experiencing it whenever a shadow stepped into the garden at night and went up the iron staircase.

It was impossible to get back to sleep. I dressed and went out to go walking in Vieux-Québec. The moon was full and in the sort of swamp that seemed to be present deep in my soul, I could sense the movement of murky things to which I couldn't even give a name.

I went up the lane that led to rue Saint-Denis, then I climbed the grassy slope to the walls of the Citadelle. From there, if I turned around I could see a light on the upper floor of the rust-coloured brick house where Kim and I lived, at the end of avenue

Sainte-Geneviève. It wasn't summer yet and the cool air was making me shiver.

The night was just beginning. Between the illuminated towers of the big hotels west of the Parliament and the green and yellow diadem crowning the Château Frontenac along the St. Lawrence, there was evidence of nightlife in the lit-up windows, the car headlights pouring onto the streets, and the moonlight shimmering on the tin roofs. Kim had told me one day that in Manichean belief, the moon was considered to be a ship that had the mission of once a month taking on board the final spark of life of those who were about to die and transporting it to the sun, thereby preventing it from being lost forever.

It was about that legend, and about my brother who had recently died, that I was thinking as I walked along the star-shaped perimeter of the Citadelle. Along the way I crossed a narrow metal footbridge that gave access to the Plains of Abraham where I often went walking, but then a sudden craving for a sandwich in a restaurant on rue Saint-Jean made me veer to the right and onto the close-cropped grass path that wound its way along the tops of the walls.

As the path was lit only by the moon I was careful where I set my feet, because there were some embrasures to step over. When I got to the Porte Saint-Louis I thought I heard a sound, but I ignored it. I went down three steps to an open-air enclosure that was lined on two sides by turrets and crenellated walls, then I suddenly realized that there were people around me. Some were embracing in the corners; others were lying on sheets of cardboard or old mattresses; still others were sitting, wrapped in blankets and holding a bottle between their knees. Some turned their heads in my direction and I could feel their gazes bore into my back while I quickly left the enclosure. I was nearly at the exit when a broad silhouette blocked my way and something like a knife or a syringe flashed in the moonlight.

A low, gravelly voice ordered: "Hand over your money!"

A threatening gesture accompanied the order. I took my wallet from the back pocket of my jeans and the individual grabbed it from my hands. I could just make out his features: his face was square and bearded and he had a tuque pulled over his ears.

He held up my paper money. "See, we just take the cash. We don't take your ID or credit cards. We aren't thieves, we're unemployed, and on top of that we live on the street. See, this is our home so we charge a right of way, okay?"

I had a lump in my throat. I simply gestured that I understood. When he handed back my wallet, though, I found the strength to ask:

"Couldn't you leave me a little?"

"What for?"

"Because . . . I was on my way to rue Saint-Jean and I was intending to get a sandwich somewhere."

"What kind?"

"Ham with lettuce and mayonnaise, and a hot chocolate," I said in one burst.

"Can't you see we've got a lot of mouths to feed?" he asked. His voice was filled with reproaches and he waved his arm to take in his companions in misfortune.

At one point he turned his head to the side and I realized that a woman was standing behind him and whispering in his ear. Sticking out her hand she shone a flashlight not much bigger than a pen onto the bills. The man took out a ten and gave it to me.

"You can see," he said, "we aren't savages."

"Thanks," I said. I slipped the money into the pocket of my jeans.

"And next time," he added, "we'll recognize you and you won't have to pay."

The woman shone the light brutally on my face and I realized that this would let them memorize my appearance so they could recognize me later on. Then they stepped aside, leaving the way clear. Half blinded by the burst of light, I stumbled as I climbed the stairs to the exit, then I left as quickly as I could. I ran for a while, then I had to slow down: I was out of breath, my back hurt and my heart was pounding in my chest. I stopped and knelt on one knee in the damp grass of the path.

I hadn't got my breath back altogether when a voice from the parking lot on the Esplanade drew my attention. A conversation was going on between two people in a calèche parked under a streetlamp by the wall. I was curious about what was going on; it was unusual for a calèche driver to be working so late because the tourist season hadn't started yet.

The driver, who was sitting sideways on the front seat, turned towards the other person. Right away I recognized the rather strange Old Man who had come to see me. There was no possible confusion: his hat was like a smaller version of the one John Wayne wore in *Rio Bravo*. As for the person he was talking to, I could only make out the feet, the rest being hidden by the hood of the calèche. And as those feet were in sandals and resting on the middle seat, and were small and very slender, it must have been a child or a young girl.

Their voices got louder. I could make out a word, a bit of a sentence here or there, and after a while I'd figured out that the young person had left home and was refusing to obey the Old Man, who seemed to be her grandfather, though in fact I didn't really know.

With a shrug that expressed a certain weariness, the old man clicked his tongue, then he pulled on the reins and the calèche drove out of the parking lot and turned left onto rue d'Auteuil. I turned that way too, following the path along the top of the wall. It would probably drive under the Porte Kent and then, farther along, keep going down the Côte d'Abraham and then back to the stables, which were in the Lower Town. The horse was grey or maybe white and, as he had a slight limp, the broken rhythm of his gait in the night created a sense of melancholy.

Just as the calèche was heading for the Porte Kent, the person sitting in the back jumped out and rushed towards rue Dauphine without turning around. It was a very young girl. She had on a light-coloured T-shirt and jeans. Curious to see where she was going I quickened my pace, sprinted down the slope just before the gate, and rushed after her. I followed her to the corner of rue Sainte-Ursule, then I stopped abruptly, asking myself why I was behaving this way — I who generally minded my own business. But the girl was there, very close by, on the other side of the street.

She had her back to me. I saw her stand on tiptoe and rap several times on a window pane; shortly afterwards, the window opened and someone held out a bunch of keys. I stood on the corner till she'd gone inside, then I went closer. The house was number 19. A door flanked by two white columns. The sign identified it as a youth hostel.

Though I've done a fair amount of travelling in my life, I've never set foot inside a youth hostel. I liked to think that the young people there were welcomed by a fat woman with red cheeks who would serve them a big bowl of chicken soup with noodles in a common room heated by a fireplace, to help them forget not only the fatigue of travel but also their wounded childhoods, their divided families, and their broken dreams.

That image of the red-cheeked woman and the hearty soup whetted my appetite and as the young girl hadn't reappeared, I hurried down the steep slope that ended at rue Saint-Jean. I had my sandwich — ham with lettuce and mayonnaise — at the Tatum restaurant, because you could eat there standing up, which prevented backache, and because I knew one of the waitresses. Actually I didn't know her very well, just enough for her to say *bonjour* or *bonsoir* with a little flame deep in her eyes and to ask me if everything was going well for me. In Vieux-Québec, there were several places like that — the Chantauteuil, the Richelieu market, the Pantoute bookstore, Giguère's tobacco store, Richard's grocery store, the Relais on Place d'Armes — where I could find some human warmth and where the people, though they didn't know who I was or what I did, stood in for family and friends.

After I'd devoured my sandwich and drained my hot chocolate to the last drop, which is always slightly bitter, I went home, taking a detour via rue de la Fabrique to avoid the steep hills. The city hall clock showed half past two. The streets were nearly deserted, but on my way out of the arcades of the Château, when I stopped briefly to admire the slow waltz of lights on the St. Lawrence, I saw shadows lurking everywhere on Terrasse Dufferin, around the kiosks and in the dark corners, no doubt in search of a soul mate.

All the time I was going up avenue Sainte-Geneviève on my way home, a question was running through my head: Would the light on the second floor still be on? When I got to the house, I saw that it was.

4

The Relais on Place d'Armes

Over the next few days, I couldn't forget the Old Man. Every time I heard the usual three signals — the scraping of the gate, the creaking of the inside staircase, and the sound of the chair in the waiting room — I would hold my breath and tell myself that maybe it was him, coming back as he'd promised.

At six o'clock I would put off closing my office, hoping he might turn up at the last moment. And in the evening, when I was eating with my friend Kim, it was painful to have to tell her that I had waited in vain.

Still I went on conscientiously doing my work. I didn't balk at writing up job applications and CVs, for which I had a series of ready-made forms, carefully filed in my computer's memory. I got pleasure from doing translations and revisions, and I took special care with personal letters, particularly with love letters.

After becoming obsolete, love letters were starting to come back into public favour. To meet the demand, I had devised a special method. One that I didn't tell clients about for the simple reason that it was morally unacceptable. It consisted of inserting phrases I took from the love letters of famous writers; these phrases, coined by brains far more gifted than mine, that had survived the test of time, seemed able to move the person to whom the letter was addressed. And my apparently satisfied clientele kept growing.

The Old Man didn't show up all week and as the days passed, my curiosity kept growing. On Saturday morning, when Kim was still asleep, I went out to look for my strange visitor.

First of all I headed for the Esplanade, because that was where the drivers parked their calèches as they waited their turn to approach customers on Place d'Armes. At the top of rue d'Auteuil I felt a pang as I walked past the house with the green wood trim where René Lévesque had lived; spring was everywhere in the air and it seemed particularly unfair that this man wasn't here to enjoy it, this man who so loved life and who had created in the soul of Quebeckers a hope much brighter than all the springtimes in the world.

The Old Man's calèche was not on the Esplanade. I continued down the street, lured for a moment by the blue-tinged curves of the Laurentians which stood out in the distance, then I turned right onto rue Sainte-Anne. From there I could have made my way to Place d'Armes with my eyes shut, guided only by the smell of horse manure, because the street was the obligatory route for all the calèches.

A glance at the line of calèches parked along the sidewalk on the right, near the old Court House, told me that the Old Man's wasn't there. It occurred to me then that old Marie might be able to help me. Marie was a waitress, and I'd known her since the far-off time when I'd come to Quebec City from my village near the American border to study literature at Laval University. She worked at the Relais on Place d'Armes; it was nearby, in the big building with a bright red roof, so I went in.

The restaurant was divided into two sections: a double row of booths and a long counter. Old Marie was standing behind the counter over a steaming cup of coffee and she was wearing her own special smile. I don't know how she did it, but she could always see me coming. When I got there my coffee was already poured, the milk and sugar were next to the cup, and she was smiling that little knowing smile.

She had a white cap on her red hair and she was leaning on the counter with a book in her hand. I sat on a stool facing her, added milk and sugar, then sipped my coffee. The book was a novel, Richard Ford's *Wildlife*, and judging by the paper napkin that she always used as a bookmark, she was well into it.

"Do you want something to eat?" she asked.

"No, thanks," I replied. "But the coffee's very good."

"How is the writing going?"

"Not too badly."

She didn't know what I wrote and probably didn't know that public writers existed. It was one of those things we never talked about and, as far as I was concerned, it was enough that she was so kind as to ask about my work.

I said: "You've nearly finished your book . . ."

"Yes," she said. "Now I just read a page or two at a time because I don't want it ever to end."

"You like it that much?"

"It's fantastic! Why are you laughing?"

"Because I would have said the same thing."

Ford's novel was one of my favourites. It is set in Great Falls,

Montana, during a summer when the whole area was devastated by forest fires. The narrator was a young boy. That summer, everything was going wrong: his father had lost his job and had to leave home to look for work; then his mother, who was usually so reasonable, fell in love with another man. Not a very original story, but it was told without one unnecessary word and, most of all, without resorting to psychology or sociology or the loathsome interior monologue. The author stayed with the concrete and he described the forest fires with such precision that by the end of the book the reader had the sense that the writer had depicted the passions that were ravaging the characters' lives. It was totally successful, truly wonderful.

Richard Ford was one of the writers I reread now and then in the hope of improving what I called my "little music" — I mean my own writing. I also read Modiano, Carver, Gabrielle Roy, Emmanuel Bove, Rilke, Brautigan, Chandler, and several other writers who had in common a way of writing that was both simple and harmonious.

Seeing that old Marie shared my tastes pleased me so much that I nearly forgot why I'd come. As I was on my way out I went back to ask if she'd noticed a new calèche driver.

"An old man with a strange hat," I told her.

She thought for a few moments, then said: "I've seen him, but he isn't new. He was around in the old days. It's just that you've forgotten; your memory's playing tricks on you. Besides, he looks a little like you . . . Don't you think so?"

"Not really . . . Do you remember his name by any chance?"

While she was trying to recall it, her eyes suddenly misty, I began to think that maybe she wasn't so far from the truth, because the Old Man did resemble my father: a long thin face with grey-blue eyes that contained a hint of melancholy.

"No," she said, "I can't think of it."

"How could I find out?"

"There may be a way . . ."

The sentence hung there and Marie, smiling faintly, pretended to go back to her reading. Finally I asked: "What's that?"

"All the drivers have to fill out a form when they apply for their permit. That form is in some filing cabinet at City Hall."

"And you think I'd be able to see it?"

"I'm sure that you couldn't, but I could; I know someone."

"You'd do that?"

"Of course. In memory of the good old days!"

When she said "the good old days," with her shy smile, old Marie was referring to the 1960s, when the university was still located in Vieux-Québec and, in the cafés and clubs in particular, you could feel a wind of freedom that heralded the collapse of some of the old values. Back then my life had been carefree, if not happy. Still, I didn't miss that period, experience having taught me to be wary of nostalgia and that it was wiser to enjoy the present day as much as possible. The problem was, I couldn't always do that.

5

Meeting in a Bookstore

Every year, in the house where I lived with Kim, three infallible signs announced the return of spring.

First of all, Pretty Cat went back to her place in what we called the Cats' Tree. Though we called it a tree, it was actually a Virginia Creeper that was as old as the house. Its branches covered the entire surface of the brick wall on the garden side. Half a dozen small boards had been affixed to the lowest branches at various heights and the neighbourhood toms who were courting Pretty Cat would come and perch there; she had her own reserved place on the top board.

Secondly, a vagabond, a more-or-less philosopher who always spent the winter in Key West, whom we'd dubbed The Watchman, had come back to Vieux-Québec. As usual, he was occupying my Volkswagen minivan, which was generally parked at the top of rue

Saint-Denis; he thought of the Volks as his personal address.

Thirdly, those clients who came to see me about private letters, no doubt feeling the need to resume relationships that had been interrupted by winter, found their way back to my office. Most of them were ordinary people and I was glad to see them.

My appointment book was filling up. At the slightest opportunity, though, I'd go for a walk in the neighbourhood, leaving a note on the garden gate to explain my absence. The Old Man's thin silhouette still filled my mind but, as Marie was trying to track him down, I was obliged to wait till I heard from her. I didn't want her to think I was badgering her, so I avoided Place d'Armes and the surrounding area. What I didn't deny myself, though, was checking out the bookstores; I looked for collections of letters for my work, or for novels that I read for the "little music," or to learn how to live, or quite simply for the pleasure of exploring another universe.

I went into a bookstore on rue de la Fabrique. Without even glancing at the current bestsellers, I headed for the American literature section. As I was passing the shelves that covered the wall on the right, a word leaped to my eyes, then disappeared at once: the word MOTHER. When books are standing close to one another, it's hard to read the titles, so it can seem as if certain words are beckoning us.

I went back and took the time to search for the book that had caught my eye, but it had already beaten a retreat and rejoined the ranks, as if frightened off by its own boldness. So I began reading, one by one, all the titles that were at my eye level, until, ten minutes or so later, I found the one that had first attracted me: Saint-Exupéry's *Letters to His Mother*.

I held the book in my hands, letting the pages slide under my thumb. Because it was part of the work that I do, I gave in to the temptation to study what we call in our jargon the opening and closing salutations. In the early letters, Saint-Exupéry addressed her as "Dear Mama," but after he'd learned to fly he called her instead "Little Mother," as if from high up in the air she could only appear smaller to him.

Inwardly I was laughing at myself for having such a simplistic idea but then, as I kept leafing through the book, I fell on a letter dated 1928, from Port-Étienne in Mauritania, in which Saint-Exupéry boasted of going big game hunting and wounding a lion. I closed the book, appalled, not wanting to know any more. Reading writers' correspondence is not without risk: more than once, doing so had made me lose all respect for people who had been long-time friends and sometimes even heroes.

To console myself I went to the aisle where my favourite writers could be found and there I saw a young person sitting on the floor, back against the shelves and head in hands. Coming closer, I saw an open book on the person's knees. Unfortunately, his or her back was resting precisely where the novels I wanted to look at were: those of Ernest Hemingway, whom I reread often for the vigour and restraint of his writing, and those of Jim Harrison, not for the writing, which was a little rough, but for the freshness of his descriptions of nature.

The young intimidate me even more than adults, so I coughed to clear my throat.

"Sorry to disturb you," I said, pointing to the books that were concealed. Without looking up from the book, which pleased me immensely, the young person used one hand to shift to the left; that movement revealed the face and I recognized the very young girl who had rushed into the youth hostel on rue Sainte-Ursule. Now that I was seeing her up close, I found her looks very surprising. She had dark skin, very short eyelashes, and slightly almond-shaped eyes. I couldn't say to what race she belonged. The strange and untamed beauty of her face was something new, something I'd never seen before.

I got a little closer, my heart pounding. Once I'd calmed down, I peered at the shelves to see if there was anything new by Harrison — a novel or short stories — but I didn't see anything special so, cocking my head to one side, I snuck a peek at the book the girl had on her knees. I can never resist the urge to know what people are reading. It was by John Fante: *Dreams from Bunker Hill.*

The girl started biting her nails. A lock of her wavy hair fell over one eye. I couldn't have told her age. For some years now the notion of age has escaped me, but I saw that she had breasts, though they were so small that they barely made a bump in her pale blue sweatshirt.

I coughed again and she looked at me. There was something bright in her very black eyes that resembled anger, and I swallowed before saying: "Excuse me again."

"Now what?" she asked in a surprisingly deep voice.

"The Fante novel that you're reading isn't his best. In fact it's actually his worst. You see, Fante had diabetes and at the end of his life he'd gone blind. So this book wasn't written normally, he had to dictate it to his wife. That's why the writing is less polished, you see. Read *Full of Life* or *My Dog Stupid* instead."

All that I reeled off in one burst and in a nervous tone that surprised me, then I walked right out of the bookstore. On the sidewalk I must have looked lost, because a little boy who was walking by, holding his mother's hand while he savoured an orange ice cream cone, turned his head and watched me for a long time.

I made an effort to pull myself together, then I crossed the street and went to the City Hall hill, intending to continue on home. As I was walking past the municipal building I decided to go and check the Old Man's file, as it was taking Marie a long time to get in touch with me. On either side of the entrance, where the door was open, some employees were planting the flowerbeds and after I'd kidded around with them for a moment, I would have no trouble slipping inside. While I was hesitating, weighing the pros and cons, old Marie emerged from the building.

"So," she laughed, "I see you don't trust me any more! Did you think Marie had forgotten her pal?"

"I'm sorry."

I felt like a schoolboy who'd been caught out. And I had the unpleasant feeling that I'd spent part of the day apologizing. Old Marie, though, whose soul was certainly lighter and less tormented than mine, was wearing her usual smile. She even gave me a few friendly pats on the back.

"I saw the secretary I know," she said. "And guess what? I was wrong! The files aren't at City Hall any more, they're at police headquarters in Parc Victoria. And not in a filing cabinet, in a computer!"

"Meaning we have to write it off?"

"Hardly! I know someone else, a policeman . . ."

"You know everybody!" I said.

"Back in the old days he was a law student . . . Strange, isn't it? Anyway, the secretary contacted him by computer. If it were me I'd have used the phone . . ."

"And what did the policeman say?"

"Something weird. He said that life is completely out of joint."

"Life is *what*?"

"*Out of joint.* What do you supposed he meant?"

"I haven't the foggiest idea," I said. "What next?"

"Next, the policeman gave her an access code to I don't know what. She typed it on her computer and then on the screen we could see the forms for the calèche drivers, with their photos and fingerprints and all kinds of other information. When I recognized the photo, the secretary let me copy down whatever I wanted."

Marie slipped a piece of paper into the back pocket of my jeans and, for a second, that small gesture made me feel like someone in an espionage movie, say *The Spy Who Came in from the Cold*. After that, she took my arm and I walked her back to work. On my way back to my office, I started to think about that young girl in the bookstore.

It was obvious that I hadn't behaved very well with her. I shouldn't have told her that the book by Fante wasn't as good as the others. What gave me the right to impose my taste? What made me think that writing was important to her? Hadn't I myself, when I was young, been blown away by the ideas in one of Ray Bradbury's novels, *Fahrenheit 451*, without paying the slightest attention to his style, which I would realize thirty years later was unusually limpid?

I had to apologize to that young reader. I went back briskly to the bookstore and hurried to the American literature section, but I didn't see anyone. The girl wasn't in the young adult section either, or in the comics. She was nowhere.

6

One Client Among Others

When I got home I saw my favourite client, Maddalena, sitting in the garden. She was Italian and she came to see me regularly for love letters. Marco, her little boy, was with her. He was playing with Pretty Cat.

She was sitting on the edge of a metal chair with her back perfectly straight, and she had on a long black skirt and a white blouse that I liked because it had barely visible red and blue flowers embroidered on the cuffs and lapels. Her dark brown hair was pulled into a bun that accentuated the severity of her face.

"I'm sorry you had to wait," I said.

"Not at all," she said in her lilting accent, "I deliberately came early so I'd have time to look at the garden and the Cats' Tree and the Japanese cherry."

She was quite right about the cherry tree: the buds were about to open and the tree — which when bare looked rather grotesque, with its trunk that was shaped like an elephant's foot — would soon become a huge basket of pink blossoms.

Before going up to my office, she asked Marco if he would rather come with us or stay in the garden.

"I'll stay with the *gatta*," he said without hesitating.

"All right, but stay in the garden, understand?" his mother ordered.

"Yes," he said. He sat on a chair and Pretty Cat jumped onto his lap.

"You can feed her," I said. "In the shed there's a bag of kibble and two blue plastic bowls. But don't give her too much: take a fistful of kibble in each hand."

"Do I put a handful in each bowl?"

"No. Put them both in one bowl and put water in the other. See the water tap over there?"

To show that he understood the boy nodded twice, once for the kibble and once for the water, then he started to pet Pretty Cat. Stretched out on his lap, she turned comically onto her back with her paws in the air. Maddalena again told her son not to go away, then she followed me up the inside staircase to my office. As soon as she was through the door she rummaged in her purse and her hand trembled when she held out the love letter she'd just received in response to the one I'd written on her last visit.

"All my friends are jealous," she said proudly. She was a chambermaid at the Château Frontenac and her colleagues' opinions about her love life were of the utmost importance to her.

During a trip to the Saguenay she had fallen in love with a man from Chicoutimi who worked in a bar. Her love was reciprocated and the man was thinking of moving to Quebec City, where she was doing her best to find him a job as barman at the Château. But he didn't know that she had a little boy. She couldn't put off telling him any longer and she was counting on me to find the words that would win him over.

In the last letter I'd written for her, which she'd insisted on copying out as she had the earlier ones, I had slipped in two sentences that Julie Drouet had written to Victor Hugo on July 9, 1843:

Hurry back, my beloved, for nothing can match a look from you, a word from you . . . Your letters are beautiful but you are worth so much more, for you are the personification of happiness.

Of course I'd changed these sentences slightly, as much to adapt them to the context as to avoid accusations of plagiarism, and my client knew nothing about my subterfuge.

Was that method the key to the relative success I enjoyed in the field of personal letters? It was hard for me to judge but, once again, the results were there, in the form of the reply that Maddalena had just handed me. So she wouldn't disturb me while I was going over it, she stepped away and sat on the windowsill, from where she could make sure that everything was all right in the garden.

When I achieve a success I always act as if it's the most normal thing in the world. So I read the letter very quickly, looking as detached as possible, but my years of experience allowed me to memorize at a glance the main lines of the reply so I could note them in Maddalena's file after she left. I began to think of what I'd have to put in the next letter.

I took a seat on the windowsill across from my client. Her hands were joined on her black mid-calf skirt. In the garden, the shed door was open and you could see young Marco's back as he bent over the bag of kibble. Pretty Cat was clinging to his shoulder. Everything was normal and Maddalena looked at me with a smile.

"It's a good letter, isn't it?"

"Yes," I said. "It's quite encouraging."

I was acting modest. In fact, though, not only was I satisfied with the results, deep down I nearly believed that my pen was the chief source of the emotions that were lighting up this woman's face.

After I'd asked her some questions to be sure I understood what tone she wanted for her next letter and what it should include, I went back to my desk to jot in a notebook all the information I'd gathered. I already knew that it would be impossible for me to write her love letter right away.

Going back to an ancient tradition illustrated at the beginning of the fifteenth century by Nicolas Flamel, it is important that public writers perform their task in the client's presence. I tried to do that, but with love letters I rarely succeeded; most of the time it was beyond my power.

That was why, if I hadn't finished my work, I forced myself to spend long hours, even days, with words turning around in my head like barn swallows. Sometimes I'd get up in the night to jot down phrases that I was afraid I wouldn't remember when I wakened.

My clients knew nothing about this turmoil. I wanted my relations with them to be characterized by confidence and serenity, and my office was set up to suggest precisely that. The walls were a peach colour that held the light and softened it. My computer and its accessories were relegated to a corner of the room, behind a screen. I liked to work in a warm and slightly old-fashioned atmosphere. My desk held only a bouquet of flowers, a pad of paper, and my Waterman pen. I wanted as few objects as possible between the client and me: no file folder, no appointment book, no telephone — nothing that could give the client the impression that he was not unique in the world.

On the wall, next to the Crouching Scribe, was a Daumier cartoon of an old-style public writer: potbellied, with sideburns, pince-nez, and a worn frock coat. Then there was a photo of Raymond Carver that I'd cut out of the *Magazine littéraire*, under which you could read:

> *Words are all we have; it's best then to choose the right ones and put the punctuation in the right place so that they will say what they're supposed to say in the best possible way.*

I took the time to chat with Maddalena. I left it to her to decide when to end our conversation and I gave her another appointment. Before she left she leaned out the window and, after planting a kiss in the palm of her hand, she made the childlike and very old gesture of blowing on it to send it to her son, and I was weak enough to think that it was partly intended for me.

7

Hockey Night

Sam Miller. That was the name on the scrap of paper Marie had slipped into my pocket. It stirred a very vague memory, a landscape of water and mist that might have something to do with my childhood.

The address, on the other hand, was perfectly clear and was located in Limoilou.

One Saturday night after eating at Kim's and cuddling for a while — an oasis of sweetness between the end of my day and the beginning of hers — I decided to go to Limoilou and try to learn something about the Old Man. Kissing me goodbye she said: "Good luck with the Watchman!"

She'd guessed right. When I got to the minivan, which I'd parked at the top of rue Saint-Denis, through a window I could see the blue-and-orange flame of my Coleman stove; the Watchman was inside.

I knocked softly on the window. No answer. I knocked again and then, thinking he was asleep, opened the sliding door a crack. He was lying on the backseat.

"Indians!" he exclaimed, sitting up and looking totally lost.

That was a gag he'd heard in a western and repeated to me now and then.

"No, no," I said patiently, "it's Jack."

"You need the van?"

"Yes."

The door slid open and I noticed that he'd put water on to boil. It was the first time I'd seen him since he'd come back from Key West. He was tanned and seemed to be in good shape despite the red eyes and drinker's nose that made him look older than his forty years.

"Coffee?" he offered.

"No, thanks," I said. "I'm in a bit of a hurry; I have to get to Limoilou."

To give more force to my words, I climbed in and got behind the wheel. The Watchman poured boiling water onto his Nescafé.

"Will you be late?"

"I doubt it," I said.

"I'll take my things anyway."

"As you wish."

Occasionally he slept slantwise in Kim's Range Rover, from which the backseat had been removed, but he had a distinct preference for my Volks, where he could use the fridge, cook on the Coleman stove, convert the seat into a double bed, and listen to music on my tape deck. He'd become a specialist in the latest American rock and country groups.

Even though he squatted in my vehicle and in Kim's, the Watchman didn't feel indebted to us; on the contrary, he felt that his presence kept prowlers away, particularly those around the Porte Saint-Louis, and in return for that service he often asked for money. I was fond of him in spite of everything, because he had novel ideas and also, since he hung out with people I didn't know, he was a good source of information.

I looked at him in the rear-view mirror. He poured milk into his coffee, added two brown sugar cubes and began to stir it.

"You're sure you don't want a coffee?"

"No, thanks," I said. "I really have to go."

He picked up the saucepan, leaned outside, and poured the rest of the boiling water next to the sidewalk. Then he put the utensils away in the cupboard and the food in the fridge. Before gathering up his belongings, he opened the curtain over the rear window. Then he stayed on to tidy up a little.

"Is something wrong?" I asked, seeing that he was taking his time.

"Yes," he said glumly. "You haven't paid me."

"I'm sorry," I said, and to get it over with I took twenty dollars from my wallet. He stuffed the bill in his pocket without a thank you or goodbye and climbed out of the minivan with his backpack and his tin coffee cup.

It was evening and the light was turning mauve. It was the hour when night emerged from the grey water of the St. Lawrence and to have a better view of it, I turned onto rue des Remparts. From there I drove down the Côte du Palais and, along the way, like a gift, the streetlamps came on. I drove across the Dorchester Bridge and once I was in Limoilou, went along 1st Avenue to 26th Street.

The address Marie had given me was a building that wasn't much to look at: square and of no particular style, three storeys high like most of the buildings on both sides of this street, which was devoid of greenery. I parked on the first cross street.

Though it was nearly dark, I had the impression that on their balconies or behind their muslin curtains, people were watching me, waiting for me to emerge from the Volks. So without hesitating I got out and went directly to the Old Man's building. There were lights at most of the windows and the curtains hadn't been drawn yet.

Inside the front door, I studied the names on the mailboxes, which were divided into two rows of three. The one I was looking for — Sam Miller — was on the last box in one row and it wasn't hard, even for me, to figure out that the Old Man's place was on the third floor on the right.

Back in the Volks, I stretched out on the seat, with my back propped against some cushions to keep an eye on the Old Man's apartment. At certain moments his long, tall silhouette appeared at the window, standing out against the bluish sparkling light from a TV set. The rest of the time he seemed to be pacing. Maybe he was expecting someone.

On the second floor, another TV set was on and despite the distance I recognized the images of "La Soirée du Hockey." Because the bursts of light from the two sets were synchronized, I realized that the Old Man was also watching the game. I turned on the radio in the minivan so I could listen to the play-by-play. It was the playoffs. I was crazy about hockey and I wasn't home watching it on TV simply because my favourite team had been eliminated during the semifinals.

Amplified by the speakers the Watchman had installed in the back, the familiar voice of the commentator flooded the minivan. Something inside me relaxed and I made myself more comfortable on the cushions, with my legs stretched out and my ankles crossed. My mind was at rest as I watched the Old Man, who went up to the window now and then, and twice came out on the balcony to look towards 1st Avenue. I was amusing myself too by looking at the first-floor TV set, trying to picture what was happening on screen from the radio commentary.

Every so often I closed my eyes.

I hadn't felt so good for a long time. I was happy to be there; a kind of peace settled inside me and, oddly enough, my sense of well-being seemed to come from the mere fact that I was sharing something with the Old Man . . . Abruptly, a series of dazzling images made me realize that the true cause was much further back: I was in my native village of Marlow, lying in a little bedroom with my brother while my father listened to the hockey game on the radio in the living room, and when our team scored I would bounce up, knowing that he was going to let me sit on the sofa with him for a while.

Nostalgia doesn't agree with me; whenever I give in to my fascination with the past, some problem comes crashing down. Which was what happened that night. While I was daydreaming, the roar of a motor nearby made me jump. A red Ford pickup truck came out of a paved lane between two buildings and drove past me, accelerating noisily. I had barely enough time to see that the Old Man was at the wheel. Five seconds later I started up as quickly as I could, but when I got to the corner of 1st Avenue the Ford had vanished.

It was unbelievable; it hadn't crossed my mind that the Old Man might leave the building through the back door! In my work as a public writer I do reasonably well, but as a detective I was pathetic! Wounded in my self-esteem, I drove slowly and aimlessly up and down the neighbouring streets. When I spotted a grocery store, I had an urge to buy myself some chocolate to cheer myself up and I parked along the sidewalk.

The grocer, a big bald man, was sitting behind his counter

watching the hockey game on a tiny TV set. I said hello and went directly to one of the aisles, forgetting that I'd spotted the chocolate display beside the cash register. As I didn't want to look like a thief I took a box of food for Pretty Cat and a teddy bear for Kim.

When I came back to the cash register a tall redhead was buying a six-pack of beer. The grocer seemed to know her well, he was chatting with her, and it occurred to me that he might also know the Old Man. To soften him up I began by talking about hockey.

"How's the game?" I asked.

"Not too bad," he said. "There's a lot of hooking and the referee doesn't do anything about it. And they're all obsessed with shooting the puck in the corner. If I was the coach I'd give a thousand-dollar fine to any player who shoots the puck the minute he's over the red line."

"With the way they're paid, do you think that would make any difference?"

"Probably not. And speaking of money, that'll be eight dollars and twenty-five cents."

"And a KitKat bar."

"That makes nine twenty-five."

"Excuse me," I said, handing him a ten-dollar bill, "I wonder if you know a man named Sam Miller. A tall, thin, old fellow . . . He lives in the neighbourhood."

The grocer dropped my change on the counter. Our eyes met and the expression on his face seemed to say that there were a lot of old fellows in the neighbourhood, that I myself was nearly in that category, and that there was no reason why he should know the names of all his customers. Still, he replied very politely: "No, I don't think I do."

"He drives a Ford pickup . . . An old red one that's falling apart."

"A red pickup? Now that rings a bell . . . Ah, yes, I do know him.

He's new in the neighbourhood. He told me he comes from a village near the border. A village called . . . what was it now?"

He shook his head for some time as if that would help him think straight. I didn't speak while he was thinking and I prayed that the grocer would come up with the name that was lost in his memory. He dropped my purchases into a plastic bag.

"I've got it! It's *Marlow!*" he exclaimed, snapping his fingers. "Yes, that's it: *Marlow!*"

"Are you sure?"

There was an uproar from the TV set that stopped him from answering. One team had just scored and it was now a two-two tie.

"They'll go into overtime," he said, adding with a wink, "That's good for beer sales!"

"Right," I said, heading for the door.

In my head another game had started; the old images had slipped out of the shadows and were preparing to attack, and I'd have to fight against that with all my might. But if you've reached a certain age, in this kind of contest the game is already lost.

8

Closed on Account of Nostalgia

When I got home it was a quarter to midnight and I was not in
my normal state. I slammed the door of the Volks and every door
in the house, I put on an old record by Cora Vaucaire that was all
scratched, and I turned up the volume as high as it would go.

It didn't take Kim long to get the message.

Lying on the bed with a pillow clutched against my chest, I could
hear quick footsteps in her office overhead. A few moments later
she showed someone out by the fire escape. She stopped on my
landing for a second, glancing in my French window, and I had
time to see that she was holding a cardboard rectangle and a roll
of tape.

She was obviously closing her office. It was what I'd been
hoping for when I put on my show, but now I felt guilty. When she
came back up and lay down beside me, I asked without looking

at her: "What did you put on your little sign?"

"I put 'Closed on Account of Nostalgia.'"

"Really?"

"Hardly," she said, "that's a joke. I just wrote: 'Closed Temporarily.'"

She kissed me on the neck and a shiver ran down my back. Then she got up and put on the Cora Vaucaire record again, from the beginning. The lyrics went:

Outside the street lights up
Orange, yellow, or canary
A cigarette smokes
Near the bed where I'm reading
Why, tonight, can I not bear
The scent of roses?

The melody went up very softly, then it hesitated and dropped down a little, then soared once more and rose even higher, and higher again the next time. It was mimicking the bluish scrolls of cigarette smoke rising hesitantly towards the light of a bedside lamp. It was one of those rare songs in which lyrics and melody were in perfect harmony.

When the song was over I turned down the volume and told Kim what had happened in Limoilou: the Old Man's silhouette at the window, my sense of well-being while I was listening to the hockey game, the images of my father in the living room, and how I'd learned that the Old Man and I are from the same village.

Did she understand why the Old Man's presence upset me so much? Probably not, because she knew no more about my past than I knew about hers, but her way of listening was unique. As I was speaking I could follow on her face, almost as well as in a mirror, the emotions that showed through beneath my words; and this already helped me distinguish between what was essential and what mattered less.

Kim was absolutely open and she had no prejudices. To her, bad habits, obsessions, and neuroses were an integral part of one's personality and served to break the monotony of life. This meant that she had the greatest respect for all her visitors, even those who came at night. She didn't like to call them "patients," agreeing with Jung that they weren't sick, and she sometimes went for a walk or a drive with them, or for a boat ride where the Laurentians begin on Bottomless Lake, whose deep water was reputed never to merge with that on the surface.

She listened closely to my account of the evening, didn't ask questions, and simply waited. But the wave of emotions that had suddenly swept over me — something that happened now and then ever since my stay in the hospital — had already withdrawn. I felt better, but because she was lying beside me, with her seductive warmth, I gave in cravenly to an urge to make the most of the situation.

I turned my back, letting my friend think that certain things were tormenting me. She moved closer, pulled up my sweater and my T-shirt, and pressed her cheek against my back; I closed my eyes, mindful of the way my skin shuddered under her breathing. Then she caressed me very gently, in slow motion, leaving it up to me to choose: to start something more I just had to turn around.

She and I had noticed that people talk endlessly about sex; as they also talk endlessly about the weather, we'd concluded that sex and the weather were equally important. Because of certain wonderful memories that each of us had of early childhood, we'd decided that sex is a matter for children. That night, as it happened, I was in the mood to behave like a child.

A moment later I pretended I was too hot. Very slowly, she pulled off my sweater and my T-shirt, and I let her go on; I could have let her go on till the end of the world. She had started to pull off my jeans when all at once her hands stopped moving. A silhouette had just stopped outside the French window.

It was a man. He was trying to peer into the darkness of the bedroom. We watched him pound up the stairs, making the fire escape shake. Then the noise stopped.

"He's sitting on the top step," said Kim.

"Do you think he didn't see your sign?" I asked.

"He saw it but he's probably going to stay till I come back."

"Do you know him?"

"Yes."

"Is it an emergency?"

"You never know."

"You'd better go to him, then."

"What about you?"

"I'm all right."

"Are you sure?"

"Yes. To tell you the truth I've been feeling better since you made that joke about the poster that read, 'Closed on Account of Nostalgia.' I hope you aren't mad at me . . ."

Leaning over me she unzipped my jeans and gently dropped a kiss there, with a raunchy little smile that was very successful.

9

To Each His Night

I had first met Kim around ten years earlier. At the time I was living alone in a house perched on the clay cliffs of Cap-Rouge. A love affair that had gone sour, followed by a heart attack that was quite possibly related, had slowed me down, and I was trying to reconnect with life.

After a long period of rest, I was making an effort to get out of the house and see the world; I went to exhibitions, book launches, art show openings, and sometimes to a bar. And so one winter night, during a Jean-Paul Lemieux retrospective at the Musée du Québec, I was studying a painting entitled "To Each His Night," when a woman came and stood beside me.

I felt her presence all the more powerfully because the gallery we were in was nearly empty. Out of the corner of my eye I could see that she was wearing jeans and a sheepskin-lined black leather jacket. My heart was beating a little too fast, so I concentrated on the painting, which depicted a man and a woman side by side, with a child in front of them, all three encased in their winter clothes and shut away inside their thoughts, looking at a snow-covered field and the threatening black sky that weighed down on it.

I tried to think of something intelligent to say. Coming up with nothing, I was walking sadly away when she asked me if I liked the painting.

"It's impressive — and rather ominous," I said. Then I turned towards the woman. She was about the same age as me, with curly grey hair and blue or green eyes (it was hard to tell with the artificial lighting), and she had on a black turtleneck under her leather jacket.

"Ominous . . . because of the sky?" she asked.

"Yes, but also because of the figures: they're shrinking back as if they're afraid of something."

"That's true, but the child's face is more confident. And look at the top, on the left: there's a little patch of sky that's brightening up . . ."

"You're right, I hadn't noticed that patch of sky. Maybe that's why the snow is so luminous . . ."

"Maybe."

"You have a better way of looking at something than I do. May I borrow it?"

"Of course," she said. A smile lit up her face, creating little lines around her eyes. "People call me Kim," she added.

"I'm Jack," I said.

She looked at the painting some more, then said that she had to leave. I asked: "Have you seen the whole exhibition?"

"No. When I like one painting a lot I don't like to go any further. I'll have to come back to see the rest."

She wished me goodnight. Just before she left she pointed out that in nearly all the paintings that she'd seen, the horizon, instead of being straight, was tilted to one side or the other. And when I showed surprise at her powers of observation, she declared, with a laugh, that she'd read that in the exhibition catalogue.

A little voice was telling me that I should ask her when she planned to come back, but I wasn't bold enough. Yet this woman appealed to me. She had a beautiful voice, calm and deep and a little husky. She saw light where to me everything seemed dark. And when she talked about the tilted horizon, it was as if she was telling me that we have the right to feel slightly off-beam in our heads.

I wanted so much to see her again that I went back to the Musée du Québec the next day at four P.M., and at the same hour every day for a week. She was never there and I wandered sadly from room to room. Or I'd sit on a bench in the main entrance that was surmounted by a dome, facing the wide windows that looked out on the snow-covered ground behind the building, and spend time watching the infinitely varied play of the snow as it fell in the night.

The museum employees would greet me amiably and some even ventured a joke, maybe thinking I was a new member of the staff.

I was waiting confidently for Wednesday, though, because it had been on a Wednesday evening that I'd met Kim. Unfortunately, when that day arrived bad weather was forecast: not a real blizzard but a good ten centimetres of snow, with winds strong enough that no one could predict what would happen. So I decided to take the bus.

I put on my polar fleece parka, my long scarf, aviator boots, tuque, and ski gloves, then I boarded the 25 bus at the corner of avenue Francoeur. I hadn't been on the bus for a while and found it restful to let myself be driven by an expert while I watched through the huge windshield the silent film of the snow being swept by the wind along Chemin Saint-Louis.

In front of me were two young people, twenty years old at most. The boy had a Walkman and now and then he'd remove one earphone and the girl would rest her head on his shoulder and listen to the music along with him. I was curious to know what the music was that they liked so much. I thought I could hear a rhythmical accented voice that made me think of rap. When the boy removed the earphone I leaned forward as if I were tucking the hem of my jeans inside my aviator boots. I then realized that what they were listening to with such fervour was not music but poems, in Spanish, by Garcia Lorca. Furthermore, the one I'd taken for a boy was a girl and vice versa: I'd got everything wrong.

At the end of Chemin Saint-Louis, the bus turned onto boulevard René-Lévesque. I got off at the corner of Bourlamaque. Snow banks obstructed the sidewalks, the blowing snow had reduced visibility, it was already a small blizzard. Just one thing kept me from going home: I had the wind at my back. It pushed me along for four or five blocks and soon I was at the museum.

Kim was just coming out; she was bareheaded and had a scarf tied around the collar of her jacket. Taking my arm, she led me to the parking lot which was filled with swirling snow.

"The Director decided to close up because of the storm," she said. "Do you live far from here?"

"In Cap-Rouge," I said, "but I took the bus."

"Let's go to my place then, it's nearby."

She pointed to a Range Rover and got behind the wheel. While she was starting the engine, I cleared the snow off the roof, the windshield, and the back window, using a little broom I'd found between the seats. To show that I knew what I was doing, I cleared off the headlights and tail lights, and swept off my boots before I got inside the vehicle.

The Range Rover started and in the time it took to get to the corner of Grande-Allée, it had got warm inside and my back muscles
had relaxed. We were going towards Vieux-Québec. At times you
could see neither the sky nor the earth, but the tires bit into the
snow without skidding and I was sure that nothing bad could happen. All at once life had become something easy and safe.

"So you came from Cap-Rouge in spite of the storm?" she asked.

"You'd said that you'd be coming back . . . I didn't want to miss
you. I wanted to see you again."

"You did?"

She shifted gears and accelerated slightly to negotiate the little
hill across from the building that housed the Ministère de la
Culture. From the way she then let her arm drop down between us
I got the impression that she wanted to touch my hand, so I pulled
off my ski gloves.

"I came every day at the end of the afternoon," I said, hoping
that my confession would move her.

As expected, she placed her hand gently on mine and for a few
moments I wove my fingers with hers. On the other side of the
Porte Saint-Louis she turned right and parked the Range Rover at
the top of rue Saint-Denis. Without locking the doors she led me
down a slippery, narrow lane that was a shortcut to avenue Sainte-
Geneviève. Halfway there she opened a gate and I followed her into
the garden of a rust-coloured brick house. I remembered that not
all that long ago, this house had been a restaurant with a terrace.

The door to the main floor wasn't locked. Before going in I took
off my tuque and used it to brush the snow off my clothes.

"Do you always leave it unlocked?" I asked.

"Yes," she said. "Sometimes people come here to take shelter. But
don't worry, the upstairs door . . ."

She took out her keys and opened it, then she led the way up a very steep staircase. The first thing she did when she got upstairs was to turn up the thermostat.

"There you go," she said, "make yourself at home. I live upstairs . . . But now that I think of it, are you expected in Cap-Rouge?"

"Yes."

"Do you want to phone?"

"It wouldn't help!" I said, laughing. "It's a cat. His name is Matousalem. I left food for him but there isn't enough for tomorrow morning."

"I can drive you to Cap-Rouge if you want. The Range Rover's good in snow."

"I can see that!" I said. "But no, it's not necessary."

I explained that I always kept the box of kibble on top of the fridge with the cornflakes and cookies, and that when Matousalem was really hungry he jumped up on the counter and then onto the fridge and pushed the box of kibble onto the floor.

"What about you," I asked, "don't you have a cat?"

"I have a little cat upstairs. She's very young. Her name is Pretty Cat. That's a souvenir of my . . ."

She broke off and made a funny face, shrugging one shoulder, and I realized that mockery or perhaps simply humour was her way of tending wounds whose pain hadn't gone away. What's more, she joked as she showed me around the apartment, then invited me up to her place for a hot chocolate. The third floor was like the second, except that the bedroom and the office were reversed. Her office contained, along with the usual furniture, an examining table surrounded by ultrasound lamps and massage equipment; a relaxation chair where Pretty Cat was asleep; a rocking chair; and in one corner, a kind of tatami mat with cushions in every size. I was curious to know what she did.

"I'm a kind of psychologist," she said. And no doubt seeing a question mark in my eyes, she went on: "But I don't try to make people normal."

"You don't?"

"I want to give them the chance to use their own abilities to the utmost, without reference to social norms."

"Are you a psychotherapist?"

"Yes, but just now I'm trying to find a method that would let me tend the body as much as the soul . . . What about you, what do you do?"

"I'm a kind of writer," I said. "A public writer."

"Instead of writing for yourself you write for others?"

I liked that way of putting it very much; it sent me up in my own estimation. I began to think that our occupations weren't all that different. When she served the chocolate, covered with a cloud of cream, I took a sip and it seemed to me that it had been a long time since I'd tasted anything so good.

In the kitchen she took a big wooden tray from a cupboard and arranged on it two oranges, bread, butter, apricot jam, coffee, milk, and cubes of brown sugar. She went back down the stairs, careful not to spill the tray, and I followed her with the hot chocolate.

"I'm bringing you this," she said once we were downstairs, "but you're under no obligation. If you don't sleep well or if you feel like coming up to my place for one reason or another, or even for no reason at all, the door won't be shut. Do you understand?"

I did understand and I was happy about everything she'd just said and everything that had gone on during the evening. When we'd finished our hot chocolate, she got up and announced that she was going back upstairs to finish some work. She wished me good night. I tried to thank her for her hospitality but she interrupted, kissing me very gently on the mouth and on the eyes.

Before I got into bed I paced the apartment, because after a certain point, happiness keeps me awake as much as unhappiness does. When my excitement had dropped, I got into bed and took only a short time to get to sleep. I woke up twice though. The first time, I was worried about Matousalem: he liked to go outside at night by squeezing through a hole in the cellar wall under the veranda, and I thought that if he'd gone out early in the evening, the wind-driven snow could have blocked access to the veranda and kept him from coming inside to get warm. I got up then and when I went to the window, which the fire escape crossed diagonally; I was reassured to see that though big flakes of snow were still falling onto the garden, at least the wind had died down.

The second time, I thought about Kim's invitation. I weighed the pros and cons in the form of a fictitious dialogue with my young brother, the one who shortly after me had also had a heart attack, which in his case had been fatal. I told him that I should turn down the invitation because most people would have accepted it and it was better not to be like everybody else; my brother replied that sex is trivial and a dead end, and that it was better to make love the first chance you got so you could move on as quickly as possible to more rewarding experiences. Like a Zouave I went back to sleep before I'd decided between the two.

10

A Footbridge Between
Body and Soul

I saw Kim several times again, at her place in Vieux-Québec or at
mine in Cap-Rouge. To my great surprise, it was the physical
attraction that predominated at first.

This was my first lovemaking since my heart problems and it
was reassuring to find that the machinery was still working. I was
glad to experience again the old sensations — desires and fears,
sweat and smells — that came from the middle of my body and
from the dawn of time. And when the physical attraction subsided,
like a fire settling down, words became more important and served
as a footbridge between body and soul. Which is why that winter is
indelibly stamped on my memory as a nearly uninterrupted series
of conversations.

By mutual agreement we talked very little about previous
loves or about the past in general. We were more interested in the

present. One night in Cap-Rouge, Kim tried to explain to me the problems she was having with her work.

"Shall I turn on the lamp?" I asked.

"No," she said. "I like the dark."

It wasn't completely dark: there was a full moon and the big living-room window opposite which we were sitting let in a diffuse light that took on a bluish tint as it glinted off the snow.

I had built a small fire. The black metal fireplace in the corner nearest the window didn't produce much heat, but it was fascinating to watch the flames — yellow, blue and green — wrap themselves around the oak logs, and to hear the fire crackling softly. Aside from that sound, which was joined intermittently by the rumbling of the furnace in the cellar, the house was silent.

Matousalem had gone outside. He was busy marking off his territory, which, because of the moon, had been invaded by the neighbourhood tomcats, and before long I could hear the strange wailing sound that he made in the night to impress his adversaries.

Kim was lying on the sofa and I was in the reclining chair. She was telling me that for a long time she had been a traditional psychotherapist who treated wealthy people through dream analysis and free association. And then there was the architect . . .

"I was very fond of him," she said in her deep and slightly husky voice. "His problem was alcoholism and I was trying to help him. It was hard. He'd been brought up by a father who sometimes gave in to towering rages and by a mother who was warm and over-protective. Whenever he was on the point of achieving some success in his work, he'd start to drink. It was a way of punishing himself . . ."

"Why would he do that?" I asked.

"His father had also been an architect. A famous architect."

"He wouldn't allow himself to be as successful as his father?"

"That's pretty well it. And to console himself, he would turn to his mother. At least that was how I interpreted his alcoholism: a need for affection addressed to the mother."

"And how would you treat it?"

That I'd been able to ask that question in a normal voice was something of a miracle, because my own parents could have been the brother and sister of the architect's and I sympathized with him.

Kim got up and went to the window.

"He was a brilliant, intuitive man. Eventually, and practically on his own, he discovered the underlying reasons for his drinking; what I did was to help him regain his self-confidence."

"And what happened?" I asked. Actually I would have liked to know how one regains self-confidence, but I didn't have the nerve to ask. Kim didn't notice; she was looking out at the edge of the property where I'd built a gazebo from which I could follow the boat traffic on the St. Lawrence.

She said: "He made some progress and he also had a couple of relapses. And then one day he won a big contract to design an arts centre in Vancouver, and he was happy and full of enthusiasm. I had the impression that he was cured. Unfortunately . . ."

Her voice broke, but as it was already slightly hoarse it was barely noticeable; right away, she regained control of herself.

"Unfortunately, the day before he was supposed to start on the plans he dropped dead of a heart attack. For me, you see, it was as if at the last moment he'd given in to fear. As if all at once he'd regressed. I tried to figure out what had been lacking from my work . . ."

She stuffed her hands into the pockets of her jeans and pressed her forehead against the window.

"Look," I said, "sometimes the heart can be tired or sick and it stops by itself . . . It happened to my brother. And it nearly happened to me."

"I know," she said softly. She was waiting to see if I was going to tell her something, but I was silent. So she went on: "I realized two things. First, that fear is not just negative but that it keeps us in touch with reality; we shouldn't try to eliminate it completely."

"And then?"

"Then I understood that a need for affection like the architect's can't be treated by the usual methods, it was too risky. I had to resort to methods that took the body into account, and not just the soul."

She fell silent and looked at the snowy landscape that sloped down in successive waves to the edge of the cliff. The light had dropped and a halo around the moon heralded a new snowfall. I didn't dare ask her exactly what those methods were. I was moved and very surprised by everything she'd said. What surprised me most was to learn how she loved her patients; it had never occurred to me before that a therapy could be a love story.

Kim didn't spend that night in Cap-Rouge. She decided to go home to Vieux-Québec because she had an early appointment the next morning. She invited me to come along and I was glad to accept, especially since, on account of my health problems, my own clientele had shrunk.

As on other occasions, I slept on the second floor. In the middle of the night I had a nightmare: sometimes images from my hospital stay would come back to haunt me. I woke up, crying out. Without getting worked up I went to the kitchen to make myself a hot drink. I only switched on a nightlight. While I waited for the water to boil I leaned on the counter across from the little window; I was watching the snow that was falling onto avenue Sainte-Geneviève when all at once Kim's silhouette was reflected in the glass.

It was the first time I'd seen her in her blue kimono. I turned to face her, wearing a contrite look.

"Sorry I woke you up," I said. That was an outright lie: I was actually very glad to see her.

"Don't catch cold," she said.

All I had on was a T-shirt, whose length was barely decent. Untying her belt, she put her arms around me and wrapped me in the folds of her kimono. I could feel her legs on mine, my sex against her warm belly. I'd have liked to caress her if my hands hadn't been so cold.

"What were you going to drink?" she asked.

"A *verveine*," I said, "but there's enough water for two . . . Would you like one?"

"Yes, please."

She held me against her for a moment and then, opening the cupboard where she'd left some things to drink and eat after my first visit, she helped me make the herbal tea. She suggested that we take our cups to the bedroom, then she got into bed with me. What I particularly liked was that she didn't seem to be in a hurry; every-thing she did, she did with total calm, as if I were the only person she had to look after.

When she asked me what I'd dreamt, I told her that it wasn't worth talking about. Then she wanted to know just what had happened to my young brother.

I sipped some tea, carefully so I wouldn't burn my lips, and told her how my brother, after working till he was in his forties at a job that caused him endless worries and stomach trouble, had decided out of the blue to abandon everything — job, house, wife and children — and move, by himself, to a cottage beside a river where all he did was putter around, walk, and learn the names of plants and birds. The cottage was in an isolated spot at the end of a narrow dirt road that was known as the Road to Infinity.

"Was that its real name?"

"Yes, I swear."

Now she took a sip of tea.

"And what happened?"

"I don't know," I said. "He was very thin, he was still having stomach pains, but he was starting to relax. He was feeling a little better and he was nearly happy. And then one morning he was found dead in his bed. His heart had stopped. That's it."

I was lying on my side with my back to her. She moved closer, kissing me on my shoulder and my neck, then she was silent for a moment, with her forehead against the back of my neck.

"Was your dream about him?"

"No," I said, turning onto my back. "I had a heart attack too, shortly before my brother's, and now and then images of my hospital stay come back."

"Was it dramatic, having a heart attack?"

"No, it was rather strange. One morning I woke up with a pain in my chest. It felt as if someone were pressing the top of my stomach with an iron bar. I didn't know what was going on, I thought I'd strained a muscle in my sleep. I got up without waking my wife and went outside. It was autumn, a cool beautiful day."

"That was in Cap-Rouge?"

"Yes. I walked for a while but the pain didn't go away. Just as I was about to go back, I saw a jogger. A tall blond guy in a fluorescent track suit with very broad shoulders and a towel around his neck. I waved and he stopped, but he kept running in place. He said that I didn't look well, and all of a sudden the pain seemed twice as bad. When I explained how I felt, he said I might be having a heart attack and that it would be a good idea to call an ambulance. Just then my wife opened the window; she said that she'd heard everything and was calling an ambulance. I sat on the veranda steps and the jogger ran off."

Sitting up in bed I took another sip before going on. Kim didn't say anything; she certainly realized that I had not yet reached the episode that came back to haunt my dreams at night. She waited, sipping tea when I did, and seemed neither impatient nor anxious.

"I spent several weeks in the hospital," I said. "One day the head of cardiology came to my room with his assistant and a group of students who were following him like a family of little ducks. After he'd looked at my file he explained to the students that one of my coronary arteries was blocked and that the best way to go about unblocking it, in his opinion, was to use a Rotablator. As he said that word, which I'd never heard before, the cardiologist drew some little circles in the air with his pen. Later, his assistant gave me more details about the treatment: a small incision would be made in my thigh through which a miniature drill with a flexible stem could be inserted into the artery to where it was blocked . . . but I apologize for all these details . . ."

"That's all right," said Kim, her voice huskier than usual.

"Sorry. What I wanted to tell you was that the operation was successful, but when they wanted to close the incision that night in my room, there were complications."

"What kind of complications?"

"I forgot to tell you that right after the operation they always insert a kind of small valve in the incision, in case they have to do part of the work again, do you understand?"

"Of course."

"That night, a doctor removed the valve and closed the incision by pressing with his thumbs for a long time on the lips of the wound and everything was going well except that later that night I was nauseated because of the anaesthetic, so . . ."

The lump I now had in my throat would keep me from reaching the end of the episode. I stopped long enough to finish my tea.

"So then," I went on, "when I felt as if I was going to vomit, I pulled the alarm bell and I could hear the nurse running down the corridor. She knew that when I vomited the spasms would reopen the incision and that she'd have to hurry before bright red blood spurted from the artery and spattered the sheets. Unfortunately, another patient who'd just been operated on was nauseated that night too and there was just one nurse for the two of us. The evening was filled with ringing bells and frantic racing down the corridor. I can't forget the racing and the bloodstains on the sheets, and they come back in my dreams now and then. And that's it."

Towards the end of my account I became agitated. To calm me, Kim rubbed my back. That comforted me and made me smile; it was exactly what my mother used to do when I was a child, but I didn't mention that.

Our conversation was over for that day. It started up again a few days later. The circumstances were different, as were the words, but the result was the same: at the end of the winter our desire to be together was so powerful that I left the little house in Cap-Rouge for good and moved into Kim's.

My one regret, which was tremendous, was abandoning Matousalem, who was too old to get used to an unknown territory. Fortunately, the new tenants were fond of him and swore that they'd see he was comfortable and respect his habits and his slightest whims.

11

The Second Visit

I attached the greatest importance to love letters, and when I wrote three or four in a week I felt that I hadn't wasted my time.

That week I'd already exceeded that number and it was only Thursday, so I took a half-day off. Instead of doing any serious work I gave myself the luxury of reading some epistolary books whose style was too refined for me to consider putting excerpts into letters for my clients. For example, these words written in the early 1920s by Katherine Mansfield:

> *The air smells faintly of tangerines with a hint of nutmeg . . . I think of you often. Especially in the evening when I am on my balcony and it is too dark to write or to do anything but wait for the stars . . . One feels partly insubstantial, sitting there like a*

shadow on the threshold of one's person while the dark tide is coming in.

After that I gave in to one of my quirks: studying the French translation of an American novel. I had long since observed that a "made in France" translation of a passage that featured baseball or football would be full of inaccuracies and even misinterpretations.

This reading was getting on my nerves a little, so I stopped. To relax my back I stood up and glanced outside at the garden where the Japanese cherry tree was in bloom. In the heat of the sun the buds had burst open and the entire tree had become a giant bouquet of pink flowers. Already the petals were spilling not only into the garden but also on the other side of the honeysuckle hedge, onto the sidewalk, and along avenue Sainte-Geneviève where the west wind would carry them far away.

Lost in thought, I heard but paid no attention to the creaking of the gate, footsteps on the inside staircase, and then outside my office door. Realizing that it was a client, I was briefly annoyed because I didn't feel like going back to work . . . And then, suddenly, I realized my mistake. I recognized those footsteps. I'd been hoping to hear them again for a long time!

I waited till I regained my calm, then I opened the door. It was the Old Man. He was still wearing his peculiar hat and his military-looking raincoat.

"Hello," I said.

He didn't reply and I stepped aside to let him in. I pointed to the armchair and he sat in it and crossed his legs, putting his hat on his knees.

"You don't recognize me?" he asked.

"Of course I do," I said. "You want to write a letter to your wife."

"That's right."

He seemed satisfied. To take advantage of his good mood, and to keep him from getting away as he'd done the first time, I decided to adopt a more authoritarian attitude. Taking my writing pad and pen from the drawer, I asked abruptly: "How would you like to begin your letter?"

"Excuse me?"

"Do you want to begin with 'My dear wife,' or 'My dear,' or would you prefer to address her by name?"

"I prefer 'My wife.'"

"As you wish," I said, and I repeated the two words out loud as I wrote them. It's a trick that everyone in the profession knows about: you repeat the client's last words, thereby giving them an official character, and usually the client feels obliged to add something.

But the Old Man didn't add a word. His silence refuted my fine theory. Though I repeated "My wife" two or three times, leaving the second word in the air between us like a drawbridge, he showed no reaction. In fact it struck me that he was beginning to wonder if I was normal.

I tried to regain the initiative.

"So what do we say to your wife?"

He took his hat and stood up abruptly. I was sure that, driven by a sudden impulse, he was about to walk out again. Instead, what he did was go to the window and, still holding on to his hat, gesture vaguely towards the garden. I joined him, thinking he wanted to show me something specific, but he repeated his gesture and I realized that he was thinking about everything in the garden: the soft green of the leaves, the blend of shadow and sunlight, the magnificence of the cherry tree in bloom, the sparkling light on the foliage.

"We tell her about all that," said the Old Man.

"We tell her that spring arrived here a while ago and that you miss her?"

"Exactly."

I went back to my desk, with a few sentences already in my head. I began the letter with these words: "Ever since spring arrived I've been missing you terribly."

As an ardent admirer of Ernest Hemingway and his disciples, the minimalists, I had a principle of avoiding adverbs as much as possible, but in this case the word "terribly" had the advantage of catching the eye; as well, it led the reader to understand that the Old Man had been missing her for some time now. And so I kept the adverb and continued the letter like this:

Today I saw a tree in bloom — a Japanese cherry tree, I was told. A wind from the west was scattering the blossoms all over the garden and even into the nearby streets, and that made me think about you. About your generosity and your warmth.

I read aloud what I'd written, paying attention to the Old Man's reaction. He didn't react to the word "generosity," which meant that I was on the right track. Still, since I didn't know his wife, it would be best to avoid terms that were too precise. He still hadn't told me anything about her.

"You know," I said without looking at him, "the quality of the letter would be better if I knew a little more about your wife . . ."

"That's obvious," he said gruffly.

I looked up, thinking that he was agreeing to tell me about her — about her personality, her tastes, her habits. Instead, he was showing me a hostile face, and this time I could see very distinctly in his gaze the strange light I thought I'd noticed during his first visit.

In the face of such a disturbing attitude, it was best not to insist. I went back to the letter, trying to stick to conventional expressions:

The apartment is empty and sad now, with you not there. Your image doesn't leave me for one minute.

That last sentence was one that I knew by heart. It didn't seem like much but I'd taken it from a letter that Paul Éluard wrote to Gala in April 1928. I added another three or four sentences, then concluded as follows:

If one day you should feel an urge to come back, know that your place is always free and that you would be welcomed very affectionately by,
Your husband.

I tried to put some life, some emotion into every letter; without emotion, words are meaningless. In the present case it wasn't too hard because I'd lived through the same experience as the Old Man. I reread the letter out loud to be sure that I had his approval. I was not unhappy: for once, I'd been able to write a love letter straightaway, as tradition demanded.

But the Old Man still didn't react.

"Is there something you don't like?" I asked.

"No, it's fine," he said.

"It will be even better when I have some more specific information about your wife!"

I was a little upset . . . Contrary to all expectations, I saw a sly smile light up his craggy, wrinkled face. It was the first time and I took advantage of it to ask: "Do you think you could bring me her photo?"

He nodded, then he stood up and started pacing the way I'd seen him do in his apartment. Meanwhile, I copied the letter onto vellum paper with my Waterman; I have what's called a fine hand.

"All you need to do is sign it," I said. "Is that all right?"

"Yes."

I took an envelope from the drawer.

"Shall I address it?"

"That's not necessary," he said after a brief hesitation.

"As you wish."

I folded the letter in three and slipped it into the envelope. When he took it I noticed that his hands were gnarled from arthritis. After stowing the envelope in a pocket of his raincoat, he left me without a word of thanks and without making an appointment. And of course without inquiring about my fee.

12

The Writer Who Couldn't Say No

I stepped inside the Relais on Place d'Armes and as usual my coffee was already on the counter.

"Sleep well?" asked old Marie with her timid smile.

"Fairly well," I said. "What about you?"

"Very well."

Once again, she'd seen me coming. It was rare that I had breakfast at the restaurant. I only did that on the mornings when Kim, after working through the night, received a last-minute visitor and couldn't share with me the brief half hour that brought us together between the end of her work and the beginning of mine.

When this happened, she still found a way to free herself for a moment and while I was still asleep, she would come downstairs and leave little notes for me. When I woke up I'd find them in the pocket of my bathrobe, inside the fridge, or in the sugar bowl. Still, there were days when these little notes didn't keep me from feeling a kind of painful shiver of what I knew I mustn't call sadness or jealousy.

About this feeling that didn't have a name old Marie knew nothing. I hadn't confided in her. But her smile and the way she brushed my hand as she put the placemat and cutlery in front of me made me think that she suspected something. Of course she was too discreet to make the slightest reference to my private life. She had a different way of helping me.

I had told her that I was looking for phrases borrowed from the love letters of writers, being careful not to reveal how I used them in my work.

And so while I was drinking my coffee that morning, old Marie took a book from a shelf behind the counter. She put on her glasses and read the following passage:

> *The rain which has been going on for two days and one night has just now stopped, of course probably only temporarily, but nonetheless an event worth celebrating, which I am doing by writing to you.*

"That's terrific!" I said. "Exactly what I'm looking for!"

"Is that so?"

She was doing her best to look modest, but as her glasses were sliding down her nose I could see that her eyes were shining with contentment.

"And who's it by?" I asked.

"Franz Kafka," she said. She held out the book, which was entitled *Letters to Milena*. It was a beautiful book: the name "Milena" was printed in wine red and the other two words in lilac. A paper napkin marked another passage which read as follows:

I'm tired, can't think of a thing, and my sole wish is go lay my head in your lap, feel your hand on my head, and stay that way through all eternity —

"That's even better!" I said. "Thanks a million."

"It's nothing," she said. "But to be perfectly honest, I don't like that Kafka very much . . ."

"Why?"

"I don't know — it's as if he's always afraid of something. One day Milena arranges to meet him and he can't go because he can't lie to the director of the office where he works. What do you think about that?"

I nodded to let her know that I disapproved of such an attitude. She smiled and, turning back to her kitchen, buttered the two slices of toast that had just popped out of the toaster; then she cut them diagonally, put them on a plate with two containers of marmalade, and set the plate next to my napkin, on which I was transcribing the two excerpts from Kafka's letters.

She left me to go and serve some people who'd just taken seats at the counter and soon I was surrounded by the peaceful murmur of morning conversations. I heard someone complain that the forecast was for rain. I had finished eating when she came back, holding the coffee pot.

"Shall I warm you up?" she asked.

"No thanks," I said. "I have to go. I have a client who's supposed to come very early."

She poured half a cup anyway. It was hot and I only took two small sips, my eye on the clock: I was already late. After I'd paid the bill and left a tip, I rushed out, then came back for the napkin, which I'd forgotten.

"I'm extremely fond of you," I murmured to old Marie.

The sky was clouding over. I went home by way of Place d'Armes and rue Mont-Carmel. As usual before an appointment, I was worried for no reason and I had a lump in my throat. In the time it took to go up to my office and let out Pretty Cat, my client was already on the stairs. I showed him in.

He was the most popular writer in Quebec City, a thin, nervous little man and slightly paranoid. He shook my hand warmly.

"I wasn't followed," he said, taking off his dark glasses.

"That's good," I said. "How are you?"

"Could be worse. How about you? Lots of work?"

"Not too much."

He had no reason to be suspicious: everyone liked him. A novelist, he wrote only bestsellers. His books got good reviews in all the papers, they were made into films or TV series, and people were so attached to his characters and to his stories that they drove with their children to the locations to visit the sets.

Known and appreciated by all, the writer was often approached by people who wanted him to attend events that sometimes were not at all literary. He couldn't accept all the invitations, but when he had to turn them down, he became blocked. He was afraid that people wouldn't like him any more.

This time he'd again brought a list of invitations. Some had come by phone and he had replied that he'd think about them, while others had come in the mail. When he held out the list I found it hard not to smile: one of the invitations was from the Farm Wives' Association of Sainte-Pétronille, another from the Quebec City Automobile Club.

"You couldn't turn down the Farm Wives' Association?"

"No," he said. "I was born in the country. I always worry that people will think I'm denying my roots."

"I understand . . . And what are the farm wives inviting you to?"

"They're putting on some kind of brunch with wine and cheese and they invite a writer or some well-known person to . . ."

". . . to give the meeting some glamour?"

"Something like that."

"Do you want to go?"

"Absolutely not. It's liable to inflame my ulcer and, also, I'm behind in my work."

"Okay. I'll write you a letter to tell the farm wives of Sainte-Pétronille that their village is one of the most beautiful in the world, that it has a special place in your heart, that there's no better spot for watching the boats on the St. Lawrence and admiring the lights of Quebec City at night, and that you intend to visit them as soon as your work will allow. How does that sound?"

"You can write that?"

"Of course."

The strain disappeared from his face and he gave me a grateful look. I suggested a few ideas for replying to the Quebec City Automobile Club and to the other invitations. He looked very happy and accepted every one. I was surprised to see how sensitive he was, how fragile, and I thought he was nearly pathetic.

He got up, took a few nervous steps, and stopped in front of the photo of the Crouching Scribe.

"What matters," he said, "is how things are said."

"Do you mean the style?"

"No!" he said, turning back to me. "Style is something else entirely!"

"You think so?"

"Yes, I do. Do you know what Flaubert said? 'Style is itself an absolute way of seeing things.'"

He repeated it three times, emphasizing in order the words "itself," "absolute," and "of seeing." In the grip of emotion, he declared that he'd found that observation in the book section of a newspaper and that the words had blazed before his eyes like camera flashes.

"It gave me a shock," he said. "For Flaubert, style is not a way to *express* things but a way to *see*! It's not a form of expression but a form of thought. Which is to say, a point of view, a philosophy. That makes all the difference in the world! Do you realize what it means?"

I was speechless, not knowing if he really wanted my opinion or if it was a rhetorical question. In any event, the exact significance of Flaubert's definition was beyond me. Then he explained: "It means that in a novel, for example, the style is what matters most . . . It means that literary critics are wrong to go on at length about the novel's story or its autobiographical content and then just add a quick word at the end about the virtues or flaws in the writing . . . It means that they miss the essential. Do you understand?"

"I do," I said. "It's more serious than I thought."

Without meaning to, I'd spoken ironically. He sat back down across from me and observed me for a moment, not speaking.

"Do you think I'm exaggerating?"

"A little, yes," I said. "There are people who've had literary pro-grammes or newspaper columns for ten or twenty years . . . If Flaubert is right, we have to conclude that all those years of work make no sense, that they're completely wasted! Would you dare to say such a thing?"

He seemed shaken.

"Certainly not," he said after a long pause. "I'm beginning to wonder if Flaubert . . ."

"Yes?"

"Maybe he'd been drinking absinthe or something like that?"

"I couldn't tell you," I said. "Why?"

"All things considered, it makes more sense to think that Flaubert had been drinking or was overworked when he wrote that."

The question having been settled, he glanced at his watch and got up, saying he had an interview at a radio station on the university campus.

"You can't turn down everything!" he said by way of apology.

"Of course not," I said.

"Tomorrow morning, I'm going back to work."

"Good luck! Your letters will be ready in a few days. I'll let you know."

After he'd left I recalled some details he'd given me one day about his work. He wrote from nine till five, Monday to Friday, as regularly as a civil servant but without the days off. He was so afraid of losing his readers' affection that he spontaneously gave up the freedom that his work as a writer would theoretically have allowed.

I knew at least one writer who didn't care for that way of working: Raymond Chandler. I'd read something on the subject in his correspondence. Simply out of curiosity, before I started the letters of refusal I looked up Chandler's words in my computer. He had written:

I'm always seeing little pieces by writers about how they don't ever wait for inspiration; they just sit down at their little desks every morning at eight, rain or shine, hangover and broken arm and all, and bang out their little stint. However blank their minds or dull their wits, no nonsense about inspiration from them. I offer them my admiration and take care to avoid their books.

And he'd added:

Me, I wait for inspiration, although I don't necessarily call it by that name. I believe that all writing that has any life in it is done with the solar plexus.

I had to admit that I didn't really see how words could come from the solar plexus and I decided to keep that question aside for the next visit from the-writer-who-couldn't-say-no.

Back at my desk I glanced out the window and noticed vaguely that a young girl in a pale blue sweatshirt was leaning against the wall of the house across the street and seemed to be looking towards the garden. I was about to go back to work when I suddenly realized that it was the very young girl whom I'd noticed in the calèche with the Old Man and had then seen in a bookstore. I went briskly back to the window. The girl was walking away along avenue Sainte-Geneviève. Her presence intrigued me and I felt an irresistible urge to follow her. A fine rain was falling so I took my umbrella, tossed a sweater over my shoulders, and ran out of the house.

13

Go Away and Write
Your Stories, Kid!

No sooner was I on the sidewalk than I saw that the girl was about twenty metres from me, heading for Terrasse Dufferin. Because of the rain, I suppose, she had pulled up the hood of her sweatshirt. I started to follow her, reserving the right to change my mind at any moment if things got complicated. I held my umbrella in front of me to hide my face.

From Kim's house, avenue Sainte-Geneviève rises slightly and at the top of that slope you emerge all at once onto a landscape so majestic that it takes your breath away. When I saw the girl disappear at the top of the hill, I sped up. I felt like Humphrey Bogart in *The Big Sleep*. But when I got to the place where I'd lost sight of her, even though I turned in every direction — towards the Terrasse, towards the Château, towards rue Laporte — she was nowhere to be seen. I was all alone with my umbrella, facing the river, which I could just make out through the soft green of the trees, and which seemed even more vast now because the grey of the sky blended with that of the water.

For want of a better idea, I turned left and walked around the block, coming back along rue des Grisons. Then I went to see if she might be at the top of rue Saint-Denis. I looked in vain; she had vanished into thin air.

I started back towards my apartment, trying to figure out why I was so pathetic. Suddenly, I jumped: the girl was there on the sidewalk, fifty paces away, and coming towards me! I quickly moved the umbrella to cover my face. There was just one explanation: she had walked around the block where I lived.

Ten paces later I got very agitated when I ventured to look over my umbrella . . . She wasn't there, she'd disappeared again! There was no cross street so she must still be very close by . . . When I walked past a wide-open porte cochère, where I could see a row of trash cans and, further away, an inner courtyard, I realized that she'd gone inside. It was number 29 avenue Sainte-Geneviève.

I had walked through that porte cochère many times during my student days: it gave access to a semi-basement where I'd lived with two cats and whose main entrance gave onto rue Saint-Denis. One winter evening my cats, which were still young and had never dared to leave the inner courtyard, ventured onto the avenue; I followed their paw prints in the snow, but they disappeared around the corner of the first street, so I had roamed the neighbourhood all night, calling them by name, quietly so as not to waken the neighbours. I never saw them again.

I went in the entrance, which was very dark, and pretended to be rummaging in my pockets for something to throw in a trash can when I felt something hard between my shoulder blades. And a deep voice demanded: "Freeze, mister!"

Obviously I've seen too many detective movies, because my spontaneous reaction was to raise my hands above my head. That made me look particularly ridiculous because my umbrella was still open . . . A hand began to grope the pockets of my jeans, then the voice ordered me to turn around. I complied, keeping my arms up. Even in the half-light I easily recognized the girl I'd already seen twice.

"Step back so I can see."

She was pointing something at me through the sleeve of her sweatshirt. I drew back and as soon as I was in the grey light of the courtyard, she stopped me.

"You can put your hands down and close your umbrella."

"Thanks," I said, glad to have a minimum of dignity restored.

"Was that you at the bookstore?"

"Yes."

"And today you followed me . . . Why?"

"It's true," I said. "How did you know?"

"The rain stopped and you still had your umbrella up . . . It was obvious that you wanted to hide your face."

"I really am pathetic!"

I put on an irritated look, laying it on rather thick, and she smiled briefly. But then she started again right away: "You didn't answer my question."

"What question?" I asked innocently.

"Why you were following me."

"Maybe I'm a dirty old man and if I see a girl looking up at my window I rush out and follow her . . ."

"I don't think so."

"Why not?"

"Because you're so polite with me. Instead of coming closer you keep a distance between us."

"What about you, don't you put distance between yourself and other people?"

"I've got another way to defend myself . . ."

Again she made something pointed stick out under the fabric of her sweatshirt.

"Are you armed?"

"Are you scared?"

"Of course."

I said that to make her happy. She was just a little girl and despite her fierce expression and her black eyes, I wasn't afraid of her. And again, her face with its mixture of backgrounds intrigued and fascinated me.

"It's just a knife," she said.

"All the same. I'm not very brave."

"Are you brave enough to offer me lunch? I'm famished. I'd give anything for a club sandwich."

I looked at my watch: twenty-five past twelve.

"All right, but I'll have to call Kim."

"Who's that? Your wife?"

"No, a friend."

"What does she do?"

I answered that question and several others as best I could while we were walking towards Place d'Armes. She hadn't said where she wanted to go for her club sandwich so, out of habit, I took her to the Relais. She seemed very interested in Kim's work and I had to explain how my friend treated unhappy people by using dreams and word association, in addition to a battery of techniques including massage, the rocking chair, reading, and songs, which revealed the maternal side of her nature.

My explanations, already confused because Kim only rarely talked to me about her work, became even more vague when we got to the bottom of the Haldimand hill where suddenly a store window showed me an image that hit me like a knife in the chest: that of a very thin, grey-haired man walking along with a girl who in the best of circumstances looked as if she could be his granddaughter.

"What's your name?" asked the girl.

"Jack," I said, hoping that my voice didn't betray how low I felt because of the reflection in the window.

"I'm Macha. What do you do?"

"I'm a public writer."

"You write letters for people?"

"That's right."

"Love letters?"

"Yes indeed."

I thought I detected admiration in her voice, which was comforting, but I quickly realized that wasn't the case at all, that in fact she'd been showing me how clever she was: she had probably followed the Old Man when he went to my place, and by asking some seemingly naïve questions she'd got me to tell her why he had called on my services.

We'd arrived at the Relais. I was determined to turn the situation to my favour. The first thing to do was to make her talk about the Old Man and her connection to him. She wanted to sit at one of the tables that had recently been set up on the sidewalk, but the sky looked threatening so I suggested we go inside. She agreed and, quicker than me, she took the last booth by the window; she sat on the side that gave her a view of Place d'Armes.

When I called Kim she didn't ask any questions, only inquired if things were working out the way I wanted. She had worked later than expected and there was such gentleness in her tired voice that I felt like wrapping the telephone cord around my neck.

Old Marie was with the girl when I went back to my seat. She'd
brought menus and cutlery. She greeted me as naturally as if she
were used to seeing me in the company of a girl so young every day.

"What'll it be?" she asked, taking out her order pad.

"Two club sandwiches," I said.

"With fries?"

"Yes," said the girl. "And a cappuccino for me."

"There isn't any," said Marie calmly.

"You don't have cappuccino?" asked the girl, surprised, speaking
louder and emphasizing every syllable. In her voice you could
hear a boundless contempt for this restaurant that didn't take the
trouble to serve the kind of coffee she preferred.

People at the other tables turned to look at us. I felt very small.

"We have very good hot chocolate," said Marie, imperturbable.

"I'll have one," I said tonelessly.

"Me too," said the girl, after a brief hesitation.

"So that's two clubs, two fries, and two chocolates," old Marie
summed up.

After she had left, the girl started to rummage in the pouch of
her sweatshirt. She took out a switchblade and placed it at the other
end of the table with the salt and pepper, an ashtray, and paper
napkin dispenser; she also took out a book which she set down on
top of the knife. It was *Full of Life*, the novel by John Fante.

"Look familiar?"

"Of course," I said. "Did you swipe it from the bookstore?"

"No, they've got a detector at the exit . . . I had to seduce a sales-
man."

I don't know if she wanted to show me how she'd done it or it if
was simply because of the heat in the restaurant, but in any case she
pulled off her sweatshirt. All she had on under it was a tank top that
was a little too big and none too clean, and whenever she bent over,

it was hard not to look at the tops of her breasts, which weren't as small as I'd thought. Customers at the tables closest to us were ogling her, and those who were leaving went out of their way to walk past us.

"You were right," she said, "it's a very good book. I like it a lot."

"I'm glad," I said.

That she shared my opinion gave me a keen satisfaction: it showed that I wasn't yet an old wreck. I asked her what she had liked best about Fante's book. She told me that she could easily picture the characters. I looked her right in the eye while I was listening so I wouldn't be distracted by her neckline. There was one scene in particular that she liked and began to describe, but just then Marie brought the sandwiches.

The waitress hadn't forgotten the coleslaw or the olives or the mayonnaise. Her mere presence, with her white headdress that made you think of the head nurse in *A Farewell to Arms*, managed to calm the libido that was gleaming in our neighbours' eyes. Her suggestion of butterscotch sundaes for dessert was accepted without discussion.

I let the girl tuck into her club sandwich; she wolfed down several big mouthfuls, alternating with French fries and then I asked: "What scene was it that you liked?"

"I really like the old guy," she said, licking her fingers. She was dipping the tip of each fry in the mayonnaise.

"The narrator's father?"

"Yes, the old bricklayer. He's fantastic! He's got hands the size of trowels, a boxer's shoulders, he's always chewing on a cigar, and he hides his butts in every corner of the house and on the low branches of the trees in the garden. My favourite scene is when Fante, I mean the narrator, goes to get him to fix a big hole in the floor of his house. Remember?"

"Of course . . ."

Now and then, instead of looking at me she would glance outside over my shoulder. When I heard a horse's hooves I realized what was happening: it was clearing up and the calèches were coming back one by one to their posts on Place d'Armes, on the right-hand side of the fountain.

"And then?" I asked, slightly irritated; I was beginning to wonder if it was I who'd brought her to the Relais or vice versa.

"So then Fante's father is in no hurry to get to work. He drinks some Chianti and he smokes his cigars. He studies the hole in the floor. He tells his son that the floor isn't even level and when Fante, who's getting impatient, offers to help, do you remember what he tells him?"

"Yes," I said, my voice simulating cheerfulness, "I remember . . ."

"He tells him: 'Go away and write your stories, kid!'"

I remembered very clearly. That curt, peremptory remark had wounded me, even though I didn't see myself as a real writer, because it had reminded me of a somewhat similar remark my own father had made long ago when I was telling him about the line of work I wanted to go into.

Busy turning over this memory, I closed myself away inside and it was only from very far off that I could hear the steps of a horse that had a slight limp. By the time I realized that it was the Old Man's calèche, it was too late: the girl had cleaned her plate and drained her hot chocolate and now was gathering up her book and her knife without waiting for the butterscotch sundae.

"Thanks a lot," she said. "That was really good."

She got up and tied the sleeves of her sweatshirt around her waist; a good half of the diners watched her leave in her slightly dirty tank top that gaped at the sides. She was going to join the Old Man; I was so sure of that, I didn't even turn my head to check.

14

An SOS *from* Kim

One evening early in July I was at Kim's place, waiting to have supper with her. She had taken one of her visitors to Bottomless Lake for a boat ride and she'd called to say that she would be home early and to invite me to eat with her.

To conceal my jealousy, I decided to greet her as warmly as possible. She'd been working hard in recent weeks, so the least I could do was to prepare a hot bath and take care of the meal.

I didn't mind cooking. Despite my very limited knowledge of the field, I prepared the meals more often than it was my turn, since my appointment book wasn't as full as hers. Besides, women had cooked for me for so long, I owed it to them.

Kim and I had no rules, but we did have our little ways. For instance, I didn't go up to her place without being invited; I didn't want to be the one who made the first move. Like most men my age, I'd made many attempts to win over women. I had tried to seduce them with words and with flowers, I'd cruised them in bars, invited them to a movie or a restaurant, taken them South in the winter; if it happened that I made love to them, my first concern was their pleasure. But as I wasn't very handsome or very smart or very rich, all my efforts had brought only meagre results. And now it seemed to me that I'd earned the right to be a little more passive and it was up to the women to sweep me off my feet.

At a quarter past seven, I started to run water into the tub, thinking that I could always warm it up if Kim arrived late. While I waited, I lay down on her bed. Some nights when she wasn't working she would snuggle up against me while I prepared the meal, she'd tickle me or caress me, and then after supper and our usual walk along rue Saint-Jean or on the Terrasse, she would undress me, taking time to look at me because she knew that I enjoyed being seen, and then she would make love to me with a hint of authority and infinite gentleness, calling on all the resources of her imagination.

I got up to make sure that the tub wasn't overflowing. The water was only halfway up the tub, but I turned it down anyway. On my way back to Kim's bedroom I stopped for a moment at the dressing table that sat in one corner of the room. What had intrigued me since my first visit was not so much the table itself as the photos stuck inside the frame of the oval mirror. As I didn't know much about Kim's past, I had reconstituted fragments of it from the photos. One showed Kim in her thirties, with a little girl of five or six; you could also see the shadow of whoever had snapped the picture, and at the bottom of it you could read: "My wife, my daughter, my shadow."

Kim appeared with the same little girl in two other photos: one by the side of a lake, the other in a rowboat. And then there was one of her all alone and looking melancholy, in a park in San Francisco: I recognized the place because of the Coit Tower. There were some postcards too, my favourite being one from the countryside near Siena, in Italy; it showed a stone house framed with olive trees that looked down on an undulating green hill, at the foot of which I discovered — hidden so well in the grass that I had to look for a long time — a flower that looked like a poppy.

I had my nose pressed against the postcard, trying to find the little flower, when the phone rang, startling me. In one corner of my brain I noted that the water was still running in the tub, then I picked up the phone.

"Hello?"

"Is that you, Jack?" asked a husky voice that was broken into little pieces. It took me a few seconds to realize that it was Kim.

"Kim! Is something wrong? Where are you?"

"At the cottage!"

"The cottage at Bottomless Lake?"

"Yes. Please come."

"I'll be right there!"

I turned off the water and went down to my place, grabbed my keys and my wallet with my driver's licence and the papers for the Volks, and tore down the stairs. I thought for a moment, then went back up to get my pills, and ran down again at top speed. In the garden, Pretty Cat was at the top of the Cats' Tree; I gave her some kibble and enough water for two days.

As I got closer to the Volks on rue Saint-Denis, I could hear the voice of Emmylou Harris. The curtains were drawn and the blind over the screen window was open a crack: the Watchman was inside. I knocked twice on the window. There was no answer, so I unlocked the door and got behind the wheel.

"Sorry, I'm in a hurry," I said, doing my best to make myself heard over the singer's voice. In the rear-view mirror I could see that he'd lowered the back of the backseat and stretched out there. "Sorry to rush you like this," I added.

"That's okay. Nowadays everybody's in a big hurry. What time is it?"

"Eight o'clock."

"In the morning?"

"No, the evening. Sorry, but it's an emergency: I have to go and help somebody."

I brusquely turned down the volume of the tape deck to remind him that the Volks did belong to me after all, and that there was an emergency.

"Is it Kim?" he asked.

"What makes you say that?"

I was aware that he knew Kim, because he sometimes slept in her Range Rover, but she hadn't told me they'd seen each other recently.

"Just a hunch," he replied, and took the time to put the seat back up, then open the curtains and fit them into their tiebacks, which closed with a snap fastener. "Will you be back tonight?" he asked.

"That's not up to me," I said.

"I'll sleep in the garden then."

"As you wish."

"You forgot to fasten your seatbelt," he said. "You're liable to get a ticket. Tickets are expensive."

He held out his hand. Without arguing I gave him a ten and fastened my seatbelt. He picked up his backpack and his sleeping bag and climbed out through the sliding door, and I was finally able to start. My irritation was still there until I drove off the Dufferin Highway on the 73, which went directly to the Laurentians.

At Stoneham, I turned left. The lake wasn't far away and I kept going as fast as the curves and the bumps in the road would allow, trying to chase from my mind a series of images in which Kim was the victim of a faceless attacker. When I got to the road that circles the lake, I saw in the distance that my friend's Range Rover was parked in front of the cottage where she brought her patients. I stopped the Volks behind her vehicle.

The door to the cottage was ajar and I closed it as soon as I was inside because of the mosquitoes. In the living room someone had been drinking beer, wine, and cognac, and there had been a fire in the fireplace. I called out to Kim but there was no reply.

I found her in one of the bedrooms at the back. She was lying across the bed, wrapped in a flowered sheet and with her face buried in a pillow. Her stillness frightened me and I was very relieved when I saw that she was breathing. Sitting on the edge of the bed, I put my hand on her shoulder and heard two or three words muffled by the pillow: she didn't want to show me her face. I bent over her and stroked her back through the sheet as gently as I could. She moaned like a baby and I was surprised and awed because to me, from the beginning, she had always embodied strength and stability. I murmured to her again and again: "There, there, little sister . . ."

Through her moans I thought I could make out that she was asking for coffee. To spare her having to repeat herself, I suggested: "I'll make some real coffee. It'll just take a minute."

The kitchen was a shambles but to avoid making noise I decided not to pick up the dirty dishes or anything else that was lying around. There was couscous all over the counter. I made the coffee, trying to ignore certain details in the bedroom that had attracted my attention: the unmade bed, the hollow in the second pillow . . .

When I came back with the cups, Kim turned around, and when I saw her face I nearly spilled the coffee. Her left cheek was swollen and there was a bruise around her eye. She'd been slapped and maybe even punched and there was no question of pretending I hadn't seen it. My hands were shaking slightly when I set the cups on the bedside table.

"Who did that to you?" I asked.

"It's nothing," she muttered, "you should have seen *his* face . . ."

She brought her arms out from under the flowered sheet, pulled herself painfully onto one elbow, and sipped some coffee, scowling because her upper lip was swollen.

"Thank you for coming," she said.

"That's all right. I'd have been here sooner but I got held up by the Watchman."

I'd hoped to force a little smile from her but this wasn't the time; she was making a tremendous effort to say something. She would start a sentence, search for the words, then stop. It was obvious that she couldn't find the right ones. Then I heard very distinctly: "I stepped out of my role . . ."

What she'd said wasn't clear, but it definitely contained the main part of what she wanted to say, because she added nothing else, no comments on what had happened. She took another sip of coffee, then turned and lay on her side with her hands between her legs; again, I could hear the voice, plaintive and husky, that made me feel so uneasy. Now and then I also heard a pine bough rubbing against the roof of the cottage.

The flowered sheet had slipped off her shoulder, showing that she was undressed, and I undressed too, so that she wouldn't touch the rough fabric of my jeans, and for other reasons that had nothing noble about them. I lay down beside her and slipped one arm under her neck, very gently to avoid touching her bruised cheek, then I wrapped my other arm around her waist and across her chest. She moved closer, pressing herself against my stomach, and her moans became less frequent.

Her fatigue put her to sleep. Then a whole carousel of images began to turn in my head: Kim arriving with a man . . . they had a drink . . . she fixed some couscous . . . he made a fire in the fireplace . . . they went to the bedroom . . . The next image was jumbled because I didn't really want to imagine what Kim meant by, "I stepped out of my role."

When she woke up it was nearly dark. I was hungry and my stomach was gurgling. She turned onto her back and from her bewildered look and the way that she snuggled up to me, I realized that once again she'd been overwhelmed by a wave of sadness. When we are unhappy we're even more alone than usual. I held her tight, rocking her and giving her the little caresses she liked so much, but it was no good. Then I had an idea.

"Just a minute," I said, "I'll put on the 'endless tape.'"

I was quite pleased with myself. There was no tape deck in the cottage but I'd come up with a way to fix that.

I kissed Kim on her shoulder and got up, taking the time to wrap the sheet around her as I removed myself. I found my keys and walked out without bothering to put any clothes on. The little lake was surrounded by evergreens and only disturbed by the very slight wake from a rowboat. A fisherman who was trawling his line stopped for a moment, oars in the air, when he caught sight of me.

Before the mosquitoes could find me, I got into the Volks and drove it behind the cottage, as close as possible to the wall of the bedroom where Kim was. I switched off the engine, being careful to leave the ignition on. I started the cassette and adjusted the volume as best I could, then I rolled down the window on the passenger side.

Back inside the cottage, I opened the bedroom window to let the music in. To my surprise, it was too loud, no doubt because of the prevailing silence, and I had to go outside again to turn it down. This time the mosquitoes didn't miss their chance. There was no question of hanging around outside and I went back in as quickly as I could.

Now the sound in the bedroom was just loud enough. Kim was lying on her back, one arm hiding half of her face. I lay down beside her and covered us with the sheet. The window was high so the Volks wasn't visible and with our eyes closed we could imagine that the music was falling from the sky.

Just then, we were listening to "Le Petit Bonheur," and the voice of Félix Leclerc was as warm and rough as a checkered shirt made of heavy wool. The cassette, which was the long-playing kind, contained my favourite songs, the ones I'd loved the most in my life. Some were well known, others less so, and some were so old that no one but me could know them. Some I liked for themselves, others because of the singer — when that was the case, they were nearly all by Montand and Piaf.

After Félix's song, we listened to "Les Goélands," by Germaine Montero, "Winterlude," by Bob Dylan, "Barbarie," by Léo Ferré, "Quand les hommes vivront d'amour," by Raymond Lévesque, "The Tennessee Waltz," by Frank "Peewee" King, and a number of others. Some were in French, others in English, but they all had in common an underlying melancholy or sadness.

The "endless cassette" wasn't called that because it had no end but because you never needed to hear it to the end. The listener's sadness was lessened and then taken away, long before the end, by the wave of melancholy from the songs. Which was what happened to me once again that evening, and we were both able to go back to Quebec City first thing the next morning.

On the way home, to distract Kim and take her mind off the assault, I gave her a detailed account of the Old Man's second visit. I also talked to her about Macha. She wasn't surprised at my description of the very young girl: she'd seen her hanging out in the garden and had even told her she could sleep on the main floor.

15

Acapulco

The melodies of some of the songs were still running through my head when I woke up. It was a quarter after twelve. Kim had slept on the second floor with me, but she wasn't there now.

I had held her till she'd fallen asleep, then I'd dozed for a few hours on the sofa and later on got back into bed so she wouldn't be alone when she woke up. It's hard for me to spend the whole night with someone; I always worry that if I move even slightly, it will keep the other person awake.

I heard sounds from the bathroom. The door was open so I went in. Kim was staring at herself in the mirror of the medicine chest; she was leaning forward, her hands on the basin, her hair falling to her shoulders on top of her kimono. In the mirror, approaching her from behind, I saw a very thin individual who resembled the Old Man. She turned around.

It looked worse than the day before. The whole left side of her face was badly swollen, with bruises ranging from red to purple and blue. It took my breath away, but I tried to act as if I hadn't noticed, which was ridiculous; since her kimono was wide open over her bosom, I felt that I could look nowhere but at her face.

"Did you see that?" she asked wearily.

"What?" I said, like an idiot. Her sad eyes were filled with reproach. "I'm sorry," I said.

"I can't work looking like this . . ."

"That's true."

"Maybe I should take a little holiday . . . Would you like to come along?"

"Where to?" I asked, suddenly concerned, as usual, at the thought of leaving my work.

"Not far," she said. "The American coast."

"Old Orchard Beach?"

"Why not?"

Old Orchard in Maine was a nearly mythical place for me: it was where my father had taken us to see the Atlantic Ocean when I was a child. I just had to close my eyes to recapture the smell of French fries, the oompah sounds of the rides, and the fine sand beach stretching to infinity on either side of a huge pontoon on piles where there were various stands and souvenir shops.

"All right," I said. "Shall we leave tomorrow?"

She wrapped her arms around my neck and gently rubbed the unbruised side of her face against my cheek. Glancing in the mirror, I saw that the Old Man was looking younger; that was something at least.

Kim made a list of things to take, errands to run, people to notify. While she was packing and making calls to shift her appointments, I went to the bank to get some American money; I refilled my prescriptions at the drug store and wasted a good hour looking for the Watchman, whom we wanted to ask to keep an eye on the house and feed Pretty Cat.

Eventually I found him lying under an oak tree near rue Saint-Denis, below the grassy slope that went up to the Citadelle. He listened to my instructions, let me know that he understood, then extended his hand. I took out my wallet and gave him a sum that, without taking the exchange rate into account, corresponded to twice what he usually wanted to guard the Volks.

I had to go back to the bank to replace the American dollars I'd just spent because, for perfectly childish reasons, I didn't want Kim to know how much I'd given the Watchman. I felt guilty, so on my way home I went to a pastry shop and bought her some chocolate éclairs.

Early next morning we got in the old Volks and hit the road for Maine. Kim was driving. She had brushed her hair and she had on sunglasses with wide temples that hid the top part of her swollen cheek; she looked like a movie star. Now and then she smiled a little, as if she were telling herself that, after all, things could have been worse. And then suddenly the grey shadow of memories passed across her face.

"When I think," she said, "that I took a self-defence course . . . It didn't help very much."

"Once I did something a lot worse," I said to console her.

"You did?"

"It was around fifteen years ago. In the fall . . ."

"In Quebec City?"

"No, I was in Acapulco."

"Fall is their rainy season. What were you doing down there at that time of year?"

"It's a long story . . . I don't want to bore you."

"Don't worry about that, we have all the time in the world."

She reached out and stroked the hair on my neck, and I bent my head to the side to make the caress last longer.

"It was a special year," I said. "I'd landed a big editing contract: a thesis on the role played by French Canadians in exploring the American west along the Oregon Trail. I thought it would be more fun to visit the places described in the thesis while I was doing the work. So I set off at the beginning of May in a Volks as old as this one. There was still snow at the side of the road because there'd just been a storm. The *last* snowstorm of the winter . . . You know the kind I mean?"

"Of course," she said. "The storm they didn't forecast, the one that wrecks your morale . . . The one that comes when the buds are swollen and the air is mild and you're burning the dead leaves that weren't raked up in the fall . . . That one that hits just when you're feeling glad you survived the winter and tired of all the effort it took to get there . . . The one that comes when right across the territory of Quebec, there isn't a single person — not even a very wise, very suspicious old man — who would dare to imagine such a backward step . . ."

"Precisely. So I drove to the Great Lakes along a road edged with snow, then I turned south to St. Louis. That was where immigrants from the East and Europe boarded boats that took them to Independence, near Kansas City, where they would embark on their long journey by covered wagon along the Oregon Trail. I'm giving you all these details because after I'd made the same trip as they had, taking notes, I came to a place in Idaho where the Trail divided: I took the branch that went to San Francisco. And I spent the summer there."

"What street did you live on?"

"Lombard Street."

"That's a rich part of town!"

"Yes, but I was in a basement. Besides, it was always damp and chilly and there was a lot of fog. I was cold and I wasn't getting enough sun. At the end of September, I read in the paper that the Mexican peso had been devalued, so I decided to go there to finish my job, and I chose Acapulco so I'd be on the ocean. Which is how I happened to be there in the fall . . . Sorry it took such a long detour to get you there!"

"Not at all, it's like the stories I used to be told when I was little. Go on — and take all the time you want."

"Thanks. So I didn't go to the tourist area but to a small hotel downtown so that I'd be with Mexicans. I was the only gringo staying there. It was very hot and every day there were storms and power failures. One night, on my way back to the hotel after supper in a neighbourhood restaurant, I took a different route home to buy something to drink. A big storm had broken and water was overflowing onto the sidewalks. I'd taken off my sandals and was walking barefoot in the warm water; it made me feel like a child again. Then all at once, in a badly lit alley, a man jumped me from behind and grabbed my neck with his powerful arm. I knew exactly how I should react: I'd read it in an excellent manual of self-defence . . . But it all happened too quickly and there was nothing I could do."

"What did it say in your excellent manual?"

"It said that if somebody attacks you from behind and tries to choke you with their arm, you should bend your knees and let your full weight drop, and at the same time elbow him in the stomach. But I didn't react at all, and in the time it took to pull myself together, he'd knocked me down and was dragging me through the street . . ."

"And then?"

"Looking over my shoulder, I saw that he was dragging me towards the inner courtyard of a house that seemed to be abandoned. I thought it was game over if that man, who was stronger than I was and apparently determined to strangle me to get at my money, took me into that deserted yard. At the entrance there was a metal gate. I grabbed hold of one of the rods with my right hand. But he started squeezing my neck even harder to make me let go."

"And then what did you do?"

Kim had suddenly lifted her foot from the gas pedal and her voice was quivering with concern. I realized then that I was getting carried away by emotions coming back from the past. My heart was pounding even harder. It would be wise to hurry and finish my story.

"I was choking, I couldn't breathe," I said. "It seemed ridiculous to die in some dark alley in Acapulco. Without letting go of the gate I managed to get two fingers of my left hand in between my neck and the arm that was strangling me. That let me breathe and I cried out. I cried out because I didn't want to die. I cried out with whatever strength I still had. Meanwhile, the man was punching me in the head and back, and kicking my legs. And just when I thought I didn't have a hope of getting away, a passerby stopped and my assailant took off."

"I'm really glad that man was there!" said Kim with a sigh of relief. She blew her nose with a Kleenex, then she stepped on the gas and the old Volks resumed its cruising speed which here, driving through the Chaudière Valley, was somewhere between sixty and a hundred kilometres an hour, depending upon how steep the hills were.

"I was so upset," I said, "and I'd been so scared that I grabbed the hand of the man who'd saved me and didn't want to let go. And for weeks to come, whenever I heard footsteps behind me at night, I'd turn around with my fists clenched. And that's all."

I fell silent, surprised that I'd talked for so long. Kim said nothing more. When we got to Beauceville, she stopped at the first restaurant and we had a coffee to help us recover from our emotions. Then I took the wheel, after I'd changed from jeans into shorts because of the heat. Kim replaced hers with a long Indian cotton skirt I'd never seen, which caressed her legs whenever she shifted on the seat. Every so often she'd rest her bare feet on the dashboard and the wind would blow her skirt above her knees. It was hard for me not to be distracted by the sight as I drove, but I did my best not to let it show so she wouldn't think about what she'd been subjected to at Bottomless Lake.

The road ran parallel to the lazy curves of the river, which flowed in the opposite direction to us. This meant that I was travelling back up the course of my memories, because we weren't far from Marlow, the village of my childhood. By taking a slight detour I could have gone to see what had become of my father's general store, the tennis court where I'd played endless matches with my deceased brother, the tall tree that in my memories stood higher than the house, the big field where Sitting Bull had been massacred by the American cavalry . . . I could have asked any of the old folks if they happened to know a man called Sam Miller . . .

I could have done all those things, but I thought that as far as going back to the past was concerned, I'd had more than enough for one day.

16

Old Orchard Beach

In Maine, we stopped in Solon, on the Kennebec River, to eat Kim's chicken sandwiches and my chocolate éclairs. After that she got back behind the wheel, and as there were no traffic hold-ups on the Interstate 95, we were in Old Orchard by late that afternoon.

Tired from all the driving, Kim left it to me to choose a motel. The one I found, which had a kitchenette, was too expensive for us, but it had the advantage of being both close to the beach and far from the hustle and bustle of downtown. Before we unpacked I suggested that we go and look at the sea right away.

It was dark green with occasional patches of grey where the light was filtered by the clouds. We had both forgotten how impressive it is to see the waves roll in and then break with a muffled sound before spreading a fringe of foam on the sand. However, a little wind off the sea that accompanied the rising tide was cooling the air. Without a word I took Kim's hand to suggest that we walk for a while and she agreed. Walking in the soft sand towards the centre of town warmed us up, but soon fatigue won out over pleasure, and Kim spotted a staircase that was built into the concrete seawall. She headed in that direction and I followed her, going around groups of vacationers lingering on the beach.

The staircase led to an alley that ran perpendicular to the shore. At the end of it, just as we were about to turn right and go back to the motel, the smell of French fries made us pause. It was coming from a snack bar off to one side and from what we could see through the windows, the place suited us perfectly, because we preferred ordinary restaurants with a counter and booths to the fashionable cafés that attracted intellectuals, artists, and journalists.

Kim chose a place near a window. Everything was in keeping with our tastes — the orange vinyl booth, the Formica table — and we had a mini-jukebox just for us. The waitress brought water, cutlery, napkins, and menus, and on hearing our accents she suggested pea soup. She called us "Honey" as if we'd been her favourite customers forever and it was easy to guess that the pea soup was on the menu to make Quebeckers feel at home.

The soup was comforting. Kim let me choose the rest and I ordered cheeseburgers with French fries, and sugar pie with ice cream for dessert. When we'd finished eating she made me listen to "Blueberry Hill" on the little jukebox. The waitress came and heated up our coffee and declared that the Fats Domino song was her favourite "in the whole world." She was a bleached blonde, all curves, with a pink apron and a cap of the same colour perched on her upswept hair, and now and then a mother hen glimmer came into her eyes, for which Kim and I were on the lookout, for different reasons: Kim because she was distraught and me because it had been my daily fare since I was little.

The waitress insisted on pouring us a third cup of coffee before we left. That night I couldn't sleep. Kim was dead to the world as soon as she lay down, but her sleep was agitated and I had to hold her in my arms for quite a while to reassure her. When she was calm again I freed my arms as carefully as I could and got up without making the bed move; I'm an expert at that kind of thing. The yellow glow from a streetlamp at the corner shed its feeble light on the inside of the motel. I took my bag and went to the kitchenette.

There was a suspicious sound outside. As the window was covered with sea spray, I opened one pane and saw a scrawny grey-and-white cat emerging from an overturned trash can. Spotting me he froze there, ears erect. With my lips I made the sound that all cats in the world — and all lovers too — take as an invitation. He went on looking at me, without moving, so I opened the little fridge and took out a piece of chicken left over from our lunch. When I went back to the window, the cat had vanished. I ate the chicken myself and that made me hungry, so I had a second piece, along with a slice of bread and butter. After that I turned on the night light on the stove and took a book out of my bag. My watch showed half past two. The tide must have been low because the regular breathing of the ocean was coming to me from very far.

My book was a novel by John Irving. Glancing at the back cover I read the words "the death of my mother," which sent shivers down my spine. Leaving the blurb, I started to read the novel, leaning against the fridge, which by chance was at just the height of my elbows. The narrator of the story, which is set in a small town in New Hampshire, is a young boy. The novel had some obvious flaws — digressions, flashbacks, pointless details — and the writing didn't flow well, but I kept reading, knowing from experience that Irving's characters would become as real as the people in my neighbourhood and as close to me as my brothers and sisters.

A few elements of the story appealed to me already. The boy's mother was amazingly lovely and attractive and I liked the way he talked about her. And he had a buddy who was quite unusual: he was very small, with a squeaky voice like a cartoon character's, and his skin was nearly translucent.

Both boys were on a baseball team. The French translator wrote "base-ball" with a hyphen, but that wasn't really his fault because the dictionaries are behind the times and they make that same error. Nevertheless, after a few pages I fell on a number of sentences that were incomprehensible. This one, for instance, about the boy who wasn't normal: "He didn't play base-ball well but as he had a very small extension he often served as a replacement . . ."

What kind of "small extension" would allow him to play as a "replacement"? I had no idea what this meant . . . Later on, when the boy stepped up to the plate, the French text read that he was "motionless, crouching, on the guardian's square."

A batter *crouching?* The *guardian's square?* What could that possibly mean? In my opinion those words had nothing to do with baseball . . . Continuing my reading, I saw that as a last resort, the boy had been chosen to play first base. And I read: "In that position he became a star. No one could run from base to base like him."

A first-baseman who ran to second and third: what strange baseball! I was starting to think that the translator lacked expertise in this area. Fortunately, the subject was abandoned in the following pages and the story took a new turn. The novel became more interesting. I stopped being distracted by the translation and my mind was totally absorbed for minutes at a time. Some twenty pages later, baseball reappeared. One brief sentence startled me.

"It was strike four."

I was appalled. Like the millions of sports fans in America, I knew perfectly well that in baseball there are only three strikes. I closed the book, switched off the night light and went back to the window. Gazing into the darkness, I started thinking about all the translators living in France, across the Atlantic, who translated American novels. They had my sympathy, because I knew how difficult a profession it was, and I felt an urge to write a letter.

I wanted to tell them that for maybe a century now there had been in Quebec a large number of people who played American baseball and football and did so in French. A French that over time had become elegant and precise, thanks to translations by radio and TV sports commentators. For that reason, I would offer them some advice as a colleague: when they were translating an American novel that had passages about baseball or football, it would be in their interest to consult one of the many Quebeckers living in Paris or elsewhere in France. If they didn't want to do that, they could simply phone the Délégation du Québec: even the operator would be able to give them the correct wording. As for me, I was available to revise their texts absolutely free, to get rid of the ridiculous mistakes that so often appear in French versions of American novels.

All alone in the dim light of the kitchenette, I was getting worked up, sounding off irrationally, so I turned on the night light again and looked for something to write with; my language would certainly be more moderate in a letter. There was no notepad but I found a paper bag in the cutlery drawer and I was about to sit down and write when I heard the sound of bare feet. The door to the kitchenette opened. It was Kim, wearing a white nightgown.

"You can't sleep?" she asked.

"No," I said. "It must be the coffee. You?"

"I slept a little. And then I started thinking some crazy things . . ."

The night light created dark shadows under her eyes that made her battered face look even more moving. She leaned against the fridge next to me, resting her head on my shoulder; she rarely did that and I felt responsible for her.

"What kind of crazy things?"

"Nothing very important."

I questioned her some more but she didn't want to answer.

"Thank you anyway," she said. She turned her head towards me to kiss me and I didn't breathe, because my breath must have still smelled of cold chicken. I led her to the window and we stood there for a while, listening to the roar of the ocean, which was getting louder; then I said: "I saw a cat just now."

"You did? Did you call him?"

"Yes, but he got away."

"I miss Pretty Cat a little . . . I hope she's all right."

She stifled a yawn. I took her back to the bedroom, holding onto her shoulders. When we were in bed I wanted to caress her to help her sleep, but she got there first. Her hands began to slip over my stomach in a movement that became a little mechanical almost right away, as if she were petting a cat. And then she slowed down, stopped completely and I realized from the sound of her breathing that she'd gone to sleep. As for me, it was morning, when the whiteness of dawn seeped in through the venetian blinds, before I managed to nod off.

There was a note written on the grocery bag on the bedside table when I got up. "You're so sound asleep I don't want to wake you up. I'm going for a walk on the beach and hope the fog will soon lift. Bon appétit! Kim."

In the kitchen I was greeted by the wonderful smell of coffee; the table was set and orange juice, rye bread, butter, and honey were set out. John Irving's novel was still on the fridge and while I ate, it occurred to me that I might be able to help chase away Kim's dark thoughts by sharing my translator's concerns with her. So before joining her on the beach, I went downtown and bought the original English version. I hurried back to the motel and packed a beach bag with a big towel and a small one, sunscreen, mineral water, bathing suit, cookies, hat, Kleenex, and the two versions of the novel.

The sun was starting to break through the mist. There weren't too many people on the beach, but I had some trouble finding Kim. She was wrapped to her neck in a blanket. I recognized her from her big sunglasses. I set my bag down beside her.

"Are you cold?" I asked. "Shall I rub your back?"

"No," she said, "it was the dampness. Now that the sun is out it's getting better. Did you wake up late?"

"Yes. And then I went into town to buy Irving's novel in English; the translation is very strange."

"Let me see . . ."

I handed her the English book, showing her how far I'd read. She turned onto her stomach, letting the blanket slide off her shoulders. She had on a black bikini and because her breasts were heavy, I had to lecture myself to stop thinking, like a kid, that at any moment they were going to pop out of her bikini top. Among the people around us were several who seemed to be thinking the same thing, but Kim didn't notice.

To get into the atmosphere of the book she scanned a few lines just before the place I'd indicated. After that she read aloud the short sentence that had hit me so hard:

"It was ball four."

She found it hard to believe that the translator had turned "ball four" into "strike four." She asked to see the translation, then she went on reading the original while I followed along in the French version. The narrator was giving a detailed account of something that had happened during a baseball game. It was the final inning and his team was at bat. As the game seemed lost, the spectators had lost interest in the play and were looking instead at the narrator's mother, who had come to cheer for her son. She was standing behind third base, in foul territory. With her skin-tight sweater, white skirt and a red scarf around her head, she was even lovelier than usual.

A batter stood at the plate. "Harry Hoyt walked," read Kim, putting on a French-from-France accent. But according to the French translation, Harry Hoyt stepped aside.

Another player came up and hit a ground ball, which was "a sure out." The translation, which read "une balle . . . hors jeu," or "offside," should have been "un retrait facile."

Then came the turn of the boy who wasn't normal. The fans laughed at him, thinking he wouldn't be able to hit the ball because he was so small. To encourage him, his buddy shouted, "Give it a ride," which meant, of course, to hit the ball as far as possible. But in French, it had become, "Fais-le courir!" or "Make it run!" and Kim made a funny face.

She burst out laughing when, to avoid a bad pitch, the boy dived "across the dirt surrounding home plate," because in French, the words "home plate" were rendered as "le monticule."

It was the first time I'd seen my friend laugh since the incident at Bottomless Lake. I laughed with her, even though part of me was sympathizing with the translator. But when she resumed her reading, I was suddenly worried: contrary to all expectations, the boy hit a line drive very hard and the ball headed for where the narrator's mother was standing, her back to the game, waving to someone she'd recognized in the crowd. I turned the page . . . I speed-read the first lines and realized that disaster was nigh. Hearing the cracking sound when the bat connected with the ball, the woman turned towards home plate, the ball struck her on the temple, she collapsed . . .

All that sprang to my eyes in a second and I grabbed the English book from Kim before she got to the passage. To apologize for my brusqueness, I said the first thing that came to mind: "Enough for today! We're on holiday, right?"

"Yes, sure," she said, a little surprised.

"Would you like me to put on some sunscreen?"

She smiled without saying a word so I quickly buried the two books in my bag and took out the tube of sunscreen. She lay on her stomach and untied the strings of her bikini top. While I was smoothing the cream onto her back, I tried to understand how I could have been so irresponsible.

I already knew, because I'd read it on the back of the book the night before, that Irving's novel described the death of the narrator's mother. So how could I have been so thoughtless as to show it to someone who'd just been the victim of a terrible assault? How could I have placed my own obsession with translation before her well-being? How could I have done such a thing to the woman I loved most in the world?

"I'm absolutely hopeless," I muttered.

"No you aren't," said Kim, "that's very nice. Your hand is soft and there isn't even one grain of sand on your fingers."

"Shall I put cream on your legs?"

"Please."

I spread some all down her legs, lingering at the places for which I had a special affection, particularly the very soft hollow behind her knee: it would have been very pleasant to linger on the inside of her thighs, where the skin is particularly velvety, but the neighbours had their eye on me.

When it was my turn to be sunscreened, things were complicated by the fact that my trunks were in my beach bag. Kim had an idea: she had me stand up, then she built a kind of miniature tepee around me by draping the blanket over my shoulders and holding the ends at arm's length in front of her to give me room to move.

Shielded by this little tent, I got out of my clothes and into my trunks without rushing. I couldn't see Kim's eyes because of her dark glasses, but she was smiling as she looked at me. I was glad that I could tell myself first that the sight pleased her; second that in the nick of time, I'd managed not to stir up her pain; and third that there was a good chance that the memory of the assault would fade before our vacation was over.

These few days passed without a hitch and as it had become intensely hot, we drove back to Quebec City in the middle of the night. It was nearly four A.M. when I parked the old Volks in its usual place.

Asleep on the backseat, which had been converted into a bed, Kim straightened up all at once. She didn't know where she was so I explained quietly that we'd just arrived, that it was still night, that she could take her time waking up while I moved most of our luggage to the house.

There were no stars and the night was dark and humid. As I walked past Kim's Range Rover, I heard loud snoring that sounded excessive and I had a hunch that the Watchman wasn't really asleep.

When I opened the gate, which made its ominous creaking sound, I heard little paws racing across the grass. I could see Pretty Cat perched at the summit of the Cats' Tree. And judging by the smell permeating the air in the garden, a number of neighbourhood toms had settled on the lower branches.

Pretty Cat came down from her perch and followed me into the house. Just before I switched on the ground floor light, I sensed that there was someone in the room. So instead, I turned on the garden light and in the dimness the first thing I saw were a pair of jeans and a white tank top that had been flung to the ground. Someone was curled up on the sofa with a flannel blanket pulled up to her chin. Her hair was black as night and her eyes gleamed. It was young Macha, and only the fatigue of the journey kept me from starting. Going on as if I hadn't seen anything, I unlocked the door to the stairs, climbed behind Pretty Cat, and left the baggage on the second floor.

When I came back down, the girl was no longer there. She wasn't in the garden, either; she had disappeared. I went back to the Volkswagen, where I found Kim sitting up in her nightgown, her head nodding gently.

"Guess who I just saw?" I asked.

"The Watchman?" she mumbled sleepily.

"No, young Macha!"

"Really?"

The young girl's name had a magical effect on her. Suddenly awake, she gathered up her things in no time at all. I helped her fold the sheet she had spread on the seat, which was unpleasant to the touch when it was humid, then she went out on the street in her nightgown, carrying her purse. After a few quick steps, she turned around.

"Is she asleep in the garden?"

Her usually calm voice quavered a little. I didn't understand why she was suddenly so edgy; I thought it was her fatigue.

"No. She was on the sofa bed."

"She was?"

"I took some things upstairs and when I came back down she wasn't there."

Kim started back to the house very slowly. She was walking ahead of me in her long white nightgown and her bare feet, and her slow, mechanical gait made her look like a sleepwalker. When we got to the Range Rover there was a slight pause in the Watchman's snoring which confirmed my impression that he was feigning sleep.

After going up to the third floor with Kim's bags, made heavier by an assortment of shells and coloured stones, I opened the window in her bedroom, which smelled musty. I heard the Range Rover's door slam and after that the rumble of the sliding door of the Volks: the Watchman had returned home.

I stood at the window for a moment, waiting to see if Kim wanted me to spend the rest of the night with her. She didn't come and I didn't hear any sound, so I went looking for her. I found her in her office, asleep with Pretty Cat on the big tatami mat where her clients could relax.

I tiptoed to her bedroom closet and took out a sheet, which I spread over her. Then I went down to my place without making a sound. Instead of going to bed, I paced back and forth in my office. I was worried, but I couldn't figure out what was wrong; some threat was prowling around me, that was all I could say. In the semi-darkness the Crouching Scribe was looking at me with his usual patience and, it seemed to me, with a little compassion.

17

The Third Visit

Several times that day my work was disturbed by the highly unusual activity of the swallows that had been nesting under the overhang of the roof since spring.

As soon as my last client had left, I went out onto the fire escape to see what was going on. The father and mother, perched on a hydro wire over the garden, were taking turns hurling themselves into nose-dive attacks on Pretty Cat who, with an innocent look, was pretending to sleep in the shadow of the Japanese cherry tree.

They were cliff swallows and nearly as colourful as barn swallows, but their tails were squared off and not beautifully forked. I was no bird expert; I'd got this information from Kim. Raising my head, I looked up at my friend's window. There wasn't a sound and the curtains were drawn; she'd worked all night again. It was late, so she would probably wake up soon.

Now and then one of the swallows came very close to the nest under the eaves, flew in place for a few moments, frenetically beating its wings, then went back to the wire where it could keep an eye on the cat. After a moment I realized that the bird that kept coming back to its young had an insect in its beak, and was showing it to the fledglings but not giving it to them. Then I realized what this commotion was all about.

Today was the day the parents, seeing that their offspring had almost attained adult size, had got it in their heads to teach them how to fly. And it was clear that Pretty Cat's presence was thwarting their plans.

I sped down the fire escape, picked up the cat and shut her inside the shed with her bowls of water and food. She meowed plaintively, looking at me as if I was a torturer, so I piled up some cardboard cartons to the level of the screen window in order that she could observe the birds without being seen. And then I sat on the steps of the shed and took in the show.

That the young swallows were reluctant to leave the warmth of the family nest and jump into space from the top of a three-storey house was perfectly understandable. In their place I'd have had the same fears. And before that, I'd have deplored being born so high up when others were lucky enough to have come into the world in a bush or a hollow tree from which you could learn to fly one stage at a time.

Suddenly I noticed that the parents were now resorting to a new tactic. They were flying in a circle in front of the nest, making squeaking cries that were obviously intended to make the youngsters think they were threatened by some grave danger. A number of other swallows from the neighbourhood came to back up the parents in their demonstration, so that one of the youngsters, frightened by all the agitation, flung itself out of the nest, awkwardly flapping its wings. My heart — like the bird's I imagine — stopped beating for a moment, but two adults came at once and surrounded the fledgling, helped it regain altitude, and led it safe and sound to the electrical wire, to which it clung.

I was relieved and impressed. I wished Kim could have been there to admire this feat. But when I looked up at her window, I spotted her: she was sitting on the fire escape, wearing a blue kimono and gesturing strangely. She pointed at my waiting room window, and with her other hand she pulled down the skin on her cheeks, making her face look thin and sunken. I finally got it: the Old Man was back and he was in the waiting room!

Very excited because I hadn't seen him for a few weeks now, I crossed the garden, avoiding as best I could the dive-bomb attacks by the swallows, and climbed up the fire escape. Before I went through the French window into my place, I gestured my thanks to Kim and she explained, with gestures from the landing where she was sitting, that the Old Man had appeared while I was in the tool shed.

I went into my office and opened the Old Man's computer file. I found the letter I'd written for him and reread the brief phrase of Éluard's that I had inserted in it. Then I hurried to show him in. Whether clients have an appointment or not, I think it's rude to make them wait.

"How are you?" I asked.

He nodded. As I'd never seen him respond to a greeting, that small gesture seemed encouraging; maybe he was in a more expansive mood.

"What's new?" I asked, motioning him into a chair.

"Nothing much," he said rather curtly.

"Did you get a reply to your letter?"

"No."

"That doesn't matter."

To tell the truth, I was deeply disappointed. It was rare that one of my letters didn't get a response, at least since I'd perfected the method of inserting quotations. But if you let a client think that you've been overtaken by events, he loses confidence in you. So I asked nonchalantly: "You're sure you've got the right address?"

"Yes."

"You mustn't worry. After all, it was a first letter. It was to be expected . . . Now we're going to write a second one, using a special method."

"All right."

"Very well. Have you brought the photo I asked for?"

"You asked me for a photo?"

"Indeed I did!"

"Well, I forgot!"

True or false? . . . Impossible to tell by scrutinizing his wizened face where the last spark of life seemed to have taken refuge deep in his eyes.

"In that case, you'll have to describe her to me in detail. I don't see any other solution."

"I'll try, but . . ."

He shook his head, as if to say that he didn't guarantee the result. I urged him to take his time, then I went and sat in my favourite place, on the window ledge, with my writing pad and my Waterman. Two young swallows were clinging to the hydro wire now and the parents were still making a racket around the nest. By craning my neck I could see Kim's suntanned legs; she was still sitting at the top of the stairs.

The Old Man lit a cigarette.

"She's good-looking woman," he began. "Tall, thin. . ."

He hesitated and I understood very well. Searching for words, trying to put them together, pacing back and forth with bits of sentences going around in my head: it was the only thing I knew how to do in this life. To help him, I said: "Come and look at something . . ."

With a cigarette in the corner of his mouth he came to the window. I asked him to come closer and to look at my friend Kim.

"Does your wife look anything like her?"

He leaned his tall frame to the side and craned his neck. Kim was dozing, with her head thrown back and her legs slightly parted. I felt at once guilty and happy. Was it because we formed a sort of triangle? Or because the Old Man resembled my father?

"The legs are the same," said the Old Man, "but . . ." He broke off and looked more closely . . . "but the skin's lighter," he went on.

"So your wife's a blonde? A redhead?"

"A blonde. A tall blonde with blue eyes."

"How old?"

"She's ageless."

For a second, our gazes met. The strange glimmer that I'd seen twice in his eyes was still there. I couldn't say if the glimmer was one of mischief or of panic. The Old Man dropped his butt into the garden, then came back and sat down. I had several more questions in mind but something warned me that this time again, it would be best to leave it at that.

"What you've told me is very helpful," I said, trying to look sincere. "Now we're going to use the special method I mentioned."

"That's fine," he said.

"We'll start the letter by telling her that all is well, that you aren't suffering from her absence at all. Your wife will have doubts then, she'll wonder if you're hiding something from her — an illness, for instance. And maybe she'll feel the need to go and see you herself."

"And if it doesn't work?"

"Then we'll write a letter in a different tone. A more urgent one."

He nodded approval. Encouraged, I took a few steps in the room, trying to recall a literary phrase that struck me as an accurate expression of the attitude I'd just mentioned. I managed to remember where I'd read it: in Chekhov's correspondence with Olga. This was something I'd read recently; I had not yet copied the phrase into my computer, but had jotted it in a notebook. I sat at my desk and found the notebook in the drawer where I kept pens and paper.

Though they'd been married for a long time, Chekhov and Olga lived apart. She, an actress, plied her trade in Moscow while he, suffering from tuberculosis, was being treated in the seaside resort of Yalta, on the Black Sea. He wrote to her often, encouraging her in her work and telling her not to be sad. The sentence I'd remembered was dated January 20, 1903.

I do not consider myself at all as injured or neglected; on the contrary, it seems to me that all is well.

They were exactly the words I needed, so I decided to use them at the beginning of the letter by integrating them into a longer sentence.

"Here we go," I told the Old Man. "We could start the letter like this: 'My dear wife . . . I am writing you to ask you how you are. As for me, I want you to know that I do not consider myself at all as injured or neglected; on the contrary, it seems to me that everything is going as well as possible.' What do you think?"

"Suits me."

"Good. Now, to show her that you're well, we'll tell her a little about what you do in a day."

"There's not much to say . . . I work . . . I drive a calèche."

"Every day?"

"No, just when I'm in the mood."

He sounded sullen. He probably thought that I was becoming too involved in his affairs.

"Look," I said, "just tell her some pleasant little things, things from everyday life, to make her nostalgic for the time when you were living together. Do you understand?"

"Yes. It's easy to understand!"

To avoid irritating him further, I fell silent. There was no question of adding a single word as long as he hadn't started to tell me anything. Getting out of my chair, I did some discreet stretching to relieve the muscles in my lower back. I glanced out the window: four swallows were lined up on the hydro wire now and as the parents were still restless, I realized that there was at least one youngster still in the nest, maybe the last-born, the weakest and most fearful in the family. Kim was on the stairs, leaning forward with her eyes wide open, carefully observing the scene.

Just as time was beginning to seem long and I'd started to worry, the Old Man began to talk.

"The finest thing for a calèche driver," he said, "is when you drive out of Vieux-Québec through the Porte Saint-Louis and turn left onto the Plains . . ."

"Yes?" I said, to encourage him.

"Right away you're in another world . . . It's as if you've gone back very far in the past."

Never before had he said so much. Sitting on the window ledge with my writing pad on my knees, I uncapped my Waterman. I was listening with the same fervour as the Crouching Scribe in his glass case.

With some hesitations, incomplete sentences, silences, and sighs and a few movements of his bony arms, the Old Man described to me the peaceful roads, the wooded hills and the broad fields that reminded him of the landscape of his childhood. He also talked about the flowers in Parc Jeanne-d'Arc, about the strollers and the lovers, and the vast view of the St. Lawrence that you had from the top of the cliff.

All these things I did my best to express in a few brief, straightforward sentences that formed the body of the letter. And I depicted as best I could the atmosphere of serenity that prevailed over the Plains in order to waken in the woman the desire to go back to her old life.

"Now," I said, "we'll have to close with something a little more personal, a little warmer."

"Like what?"

"For instance, you could wish that in her heart and in her life there will be the same peace that there is on the Plains. Something like that."

"That's fine."

His mood was more and more conciliatory, so I made the most of it to persuade him to close the letter with a very simple formula: "Your loving husband." Then I went back to my table and copied out the letter, writing very carefully.

"You just have to add your signature," I said.

"All right."

"Shall I address the envelope?"

Recalling that on his previous visit he had declined my offer, I pretended that I considered the question unimportant, as if it had been agreed upon in advance. The Old Man hesitated briefly.

"No," he said. "I'll take care of that."

"As you wish, but it won't be the same handwriting as the letter . . . Don't you think your wife might find that strange?"

"No, I'll type the address. I know someone."

He spoke without looking at me.

"If you want, I could do it on my typewriter right now," I said.

"No, I'm in a bit of a hurry . . ."

"It would just take a minute . . ."

"No, thanks. I've got an appointment with somebody."

He was already on his feet. He had his raincoat over one arm and he was holding his battered hat, and I realized that I mustn't push it. I slipped the letter into the envelope, held it out to him and, as on previous occasions, he left without saying goodbye or thanks, and with no mention of my fee, though the rates were posted in the waiting room.

When he'd gone, I began to copy the letter into my computer to add to his file, but all at once I felt a need to know with whom he had an appointment. And before that, if he actually had one at all.

To keep from being recognized, I put on my tennis hat, sunglasses, and a putty-coloured trench coat that had come to me from my brother. I laughed at myself as I tore down the inside staircase; it seemed that I was about to identify with Bogart again — minus the talent.

In the garden, I let Pretty Cat out of the shed.

Five young swallows were lined up on the wire.

Kim had gone back inside.

18

The Unlikely Detective

When I left the garden, the gate creaked like a clothesline pulley and I was afraid that the sound would attract the Old Man's attention. I looked towards the top of the lane, in the direction of the Citadelle, but he wasn't there. Turning in the other direction, I spied him walking along rue Sainte-Ursule. He was walking slowly and didn't appear to have seen me. I started to follow him at a distance.

He hesitated briefly at the corner of rue Saint-Louis, which was awash in August tourists, then continued straight ahead. With his tall stature and his unusual hat, it would be hard to lose sight of him. Besides, he was taking his time. Though he'd said he was in a hurry, he kept stopping to look at some geraniums in a window, an old-model car, a workman repairing a building façade. Then I would do what specialists in shadowing people do in detective movies: tie my shoelaces or become engrossed in a sign advertising an apartment for rent.

From the other side of rue Sainte-Anne, at the start of a very steep descent, I thought he was going to stop at the youth hostel to see young Macha, but I was mistaken. He went down to rue Saint-Jean and turned left. I did the same, careful to take the other sidewalk which now, in the late afternoon, was in the shade. It was even easier to follow him at this point; I could either keep an eye on him directly or keep an eye on his reflection in the store windows.

When he walked beneath the arch of the Porte Saint-Louis, a bare-chested young man asked for a handout. They started talking and finally the young man gestured nonchalantly towards the Côte d'Abraham. The Old Man headed that way and while he was crossing Place d'Youville, I hid behind one of the columns of the Capitol Theatre. He disappeared at the corner of rue des Glacis. I waited for a few moments, then hurried to see what was going on. To my great surprise he had already vanished. I didn't see him on the sidewalk or at the intersection where the city buses were parked.

As discreetly as I could, I walked around the parked buses. They were full; it was the hour when people were going home. But though I looked inside each bus and in the vicinity, the Old Man was nowhere to be seen. What would Bogie have done in my place? I couldn't get an answer to that question and I was on my way pathetically back home by way of rue d'Auteuil, in case the Old Man had decided at the last moment to go to the Esplanade, when all of a sudden I spotted him. He was coming out of a store that sold tobacco and newspapers, holding a package of cigarettes. I had just enough time to nip into a bus shelter. With my hat over my eyes and my collar pulled up, I pretended to be very busy puzzling out the map of the bus system.

The Old Man lit a cigarette and started along the Côte

d'Abraham. There were fewer pedestrians in this part of town, so it was in my interest to put some more distance between us. And so when he suddenly crossed the street and disappeared into a building near the middle of the hill, I couldn't immediately see where he'd gone. I quickly went and stood out of sight at the corner of rue Saint-Augustin, which was the first cross street. When I saw the door with a window on either side I realized that this was l'Archipel, a business that had been turned into a shelter for young runaways and drug users: a photo of the building had appeared in *Le Soleil.*

I waited and waited. Passersby looked at me suspiciously; some went off the sidewalk and around the corner that I'd made my observation post. I was not at all comfortable. Seeing two old women coming towards me, clinging to each other, I took off my hat and my dark glasses to ask them the best way to get to the Gare du Palais. One launched into an explanation and the other continued; they hadn't finished telling me the route when the Old Man came out of L'Archipel, accompanied by young Macha.

After the first moment of surprise, I thanked the ladies and resumed my shadowing. The Old Man and the girl went up the Côte d'Abraham and I followed them at a respectful distance, remembering how easily she had spotted me earlier in the summer.

They were walking side by side, without touching. The Old Man as usual stood lopsided, his right shoulder higher than the left; the slanting line of his shoulders led to the girl's black hair. My feelings were lopsided too: I thought that the Old Man and the girl formed an ill-matched couple that was somewhat incongruous and nearly indecent, and there was pettiness in my way of seeing them.

They stepped into Vieux-Québec and walked along rue Saint-Jean, stopping at every restaurant to read the menu. I had no trouble following them, but things became complicated when they turned onto rue Couillard, which was narrow and not so busy. I let them get a good lead and then, just as they were about to disappear around the first corner, I hurried after them. I had time to see them go into Chez Temporel.

The café was pleasant but small and generally you saw no one there but regulars. Even though I was not, strictly speaking, one of them, there was a chance that if I went inside someone would recognize me and call out, despite my disguise. I hesitated . . . and finally decided to risk it. To give myself some confidence, I stuffed my hands into my pockets and as I did so, realized that I'd forgotten my wallet! Before I left the house I had changed clothes in a hurry and I'd forgotten to take my money and my papers; I didn't have a cent on me. What a pathetic detective!

The simplest solution was to call Kim to my rescue. As I had no money and no telephone card, I went into the grocery store next to Chez Temporel, hoping the owner would let me use his phone. He was behind his counter, serving liquorice and candy to some children; he listened without a word and pushed the telephone towards me with a morose expression.

I sat on the edge of the sidewalk and chatted with some children, which didn't stop me from keeping an eye on the café with its dark green door surmounted by a rooster. Less than ten minutes later, Kim was there, breathing hard and with a glimmer of concern in her eyes. Needless to say, she recognized me at once, and my so-called disguise made her smile.

While I was telling her what had happened, I helped her into my putty-coloured raincoat, plunked my tennis hat on her head and my sunglasses on her nose, and gave her the mission of going into the café to spy on the Old Man and the girl. We would meet afterwards at the Sainte-Angèle bar on the street of the same name. She smiled and wordlessly agreed. What was great about Kim was that nothing surprised her; you could ask her anything.

Before going inside, she lent me a little money so I could have a drink while I was waiting at the Sainte-Angèle. Before that, I wanted to go back to the grocery store to buy some little thing so the owner wouldn't think I was a boor.

I waited at the bar for nearly an hour, sipping apéritifs at the counter. My head was spinning a little and a gentle sense of melancholy, which I enjoyed, came over me as I thought back to all the times since the beginning of summer that I'd behaved like an idiot by trying to act like a Bogart character. When she finally arrived and saw the state I was in, Kim ordered black coffee. Taking off the hat and glasses, she started telling me what had happened.

"Good thing I had my purse . . ."

"Why's that?" I asked, my voice groggy.

"There was a mirror in it. I sat at a table nearby with my back to them so they couldn't recognize me, and I watched them in the mirror, which I'd propped against the sugar bowl."

"Fantastic! That was a terrific idea!"

"I felt like someone in a movie. You know, *Casablanca*, something like that."

"I know," I said. "I know *ex-act-ly* what you mean . . . So tell me, what were they doing?"

"Talking very softly, whispering really. I caught a word here and there when the café was quiet. She did most of the talking . . . I heard 'cat' and 'sleep'; do you think that means anything special?"

"Couldn't say . . . And the Old Man, what was he like with her? Authoritarian? . . . Fatherly? . . . Loving?"

The barmaid brought two black coffees and I quickly took a sip to hide the nervousness that had just taken hold of me. Certain words, like the last one I'd just spoken, were destined to stir some very old emotions in me.

"Are you all right?" asked Kim.

"I'm fine," I said, rather impatient. Then I was silent, waiting for her to answer my question.

"Hard to tell," she said. "He didn't say much. He sat there, barely moving, with a cigarette in the corner of his mouth and his raincoat over his knees. In any case, he's a lot older than she is; he looks like her grandfather."

"Do you think he really is her grandfather?"

"I doubt it. The girl is homeless . . . They probably met by chance and I suppose the Old Man helped her out . . . Why are you laughing? You just said you were sad and now you're laughing . . ."

"It doesn't matter. So what did you see after that?"

"Towards the end, he took an envelope from his raincoat pocket. It wasn't sealed. He took out a letter and the girl read it . . ."

"And could you see her face?"

"Of course. It seemed softer. Till then she'd looked belligerent, as if she wanted to bite. But as she was reading it she pushed back a lock of her curly hair and I saw a very gentle light in her eyes. In fact I turned around for a better look . . . It was like black velvet."

"It was?" I said, surprised at the emotion in her voice.

Kim took a long sip of coffee, while I was doing my best to collect my thoughts. The bar was gradually filling up and the sound of conversations became too loud. We were lucky enough to have the enveloping presence of the barmaid around us and the muffled softness of her comings and goings.

I leaned across to Kim so I wouldn't have to raise my voice.

"And then? Did the girl hold on to the letter?"

"You won't like this," she said.

"Why not?"

"Well, the girl finished her reading, with that strange light in her face, and she put the letter on the table. Then the Old Man beckoned to the waiter for the bill. The waiter came, but he stayed there with them while they were getting up to go. He was standing between them and me so he blocked my field of vision in the mirror and I couldn't see if it was the Old Man or the girl who took the letter. I'm sorry."

She scowled, then replaced the dark glasses and tennis hat, pulling it down over her eyes; the hat, all soft and bent out of shape, gave her a comical look that was absolutely irresistible.

"I wasn't very brilliant!"

"It's all right. That kind of thing happens to me all the time."

"Do you want to drown your sorrow or would you rather go home?"

"Go home."

The perfect unity with which we raised our elbows to drain our coffee cups made us both laugh, but I was actually getting more and more worried. Through the fog that had taken over my brain, I could sense that the danger hanging over me had come closer. That night I had a dream that took me back to my early childhood and I woke up with feelings that were no doubt not too unlike the ones experienced by the last of the young swallows, just before it jumped into the void.

19

A Humorist

That morning, I was expecting a visit from a humorist. I hadn't seen him for several years. The last time he'd called he had another job: he was a civil servant. He wrote speeches for cabinet ministers and he'd got in the habit of dropping in to show me what he'd written or to look for new ideas.

I was a little anxious because since then he'd become a star; I'd seen him often on TV. As he hadn't yet arrived at the appointed time, I started pacing nervously past the window that overlooked the garden. The vine was growing over the window frame and a few leaves were turning red. Pretty Cat noticed me, climbed up the iron staircase though she didn't like doing so, and came in through my bedroom. From the way she rubbed against my legs, nudging me towards the door of my office, it was obvious that she was hungry.

It wasn't time for her meal yet but I let myself be persuaded to go to the kitchen. First I glanced out the window over the sink to make sure that my visitor hadn't arrived, then I attended to the cat. She had jumped onto the counter and, standing on the tips of her paws, she vigorously thrust her damp muzzle under my chin, which in cat language meant that she couldn't wait any more. I took from the fridge a slice of cooked ham that I'd intended to have for lunch and gave her half, cutting it into small pieces to prolong her pleasure. I also gave her a saucer of milk and while I was putting it in the sink, I looked out the window and saw the humorist pulling up in a taxi.

Briskly, I went back to my office. A moment later the gate creaked and then I heard footsteps on the stairs. As the relationship between us had always been cordial, I was expecting our get-together now to be friendly, if not warm. It was, however, the very opposite.

"I'll get right to the point," he declared, after extending a cold, limp hand. "I have a lot of work and I need something funny that runs fifteen minutes or so. I haven't got time to write it . . . Could you do it for me?"

I disliked this request as soon as I heard it — and his contemptuous manner too — and I decided that I'd turn him down. But I had to justify my refusal, because throughout my life I've never been able to say something as simple as, "No, that's not convenient."

"Have you got a theme, the beginning of a storyline?" I asked.

He shook his head. He was a beanpole wearing a black T-shirt inscribed "Festival du Rire," and his appearance made me think of a crow or a singer from the old days named Philippe Clay.

"I haven't got a thing," he said, and there was melancholy in his voice.

"In that case we can try to come up with something together . . ."

"I've been trying for a week, but right now I'm too tired. I've got too much work. Can you understand?"

"Of course."

"But you," he said, "I suppose you've got the time."

"Yes," I said, "but actually . . ."

He raised his hand to interrupt.

"Your work is writing things for others?"

"That's right."

"All kinds of things?"

"Yes."

"You don't specialize in any one area?"

"No, but . . ."

"Which means that you should be able to think up something funny, right? Try!"

His peremptory tone of voice was getting on my nerves, which was why I kept my effort to the strict minimum. And yet, a few seconds later, I remembered a funny piece. Something I'd read, if I remember correctly, in an old issue of *Historia*.

"Aha! You've come up with something!" exclaimed the humorist. "I saw your face light up!"

"It's just a little thing," I said, "but I'll tell you anyway. There's a dinner party at which the guest of honour is Voltaire. He's seated next to one of the grandes dames of the time, Madame du Deffant or Madame du Châtelet, and he's ogling the very low neckline of the lady, who is no longer young. 'Don't tell me these little creatures still attract your interest!' exclaims the woman, surprised. And Voltaire replies: '*Little* creatures? Chère madame, I would say that they're among the Creator's *greatest* works.'"

The wordplay wasn't all that bad, and I actually expected it would wrench a smile from my visitor, even just a smile of sympathy; he could not be unaware that a person who has just told a joke feels as vulnerable as if he's just confided a secret. But I didn't get a smile, I could even hear disapproval in his voice when he murmured: "I'd forgotten that you're more the *literary* type."

"That's not exactly the word I'd use . . ."

"Couldn't you think of a situation, let's say . . . more ordinary, more contemporary?"

"I can try."

This time, I closed my eyes. I was using a meditation technique I'd found in one of Kim's books. You imagine that you're looking at a candle flame. You focus on it while you make your mind go blank and gradually you go deep down inside yourself, like a diver letting himself sink to the bottom.

In fact it was nothing but a simulation intended to impress my client. Except that I really could see the point of light; it was a problem that had cropped up following my heart trouble and it was called "ophthalmic migraine": with my eyes closed I saw a gold-coloured blinking light enter my field of vision from the left, move diagonally across my eyes very slowly, and fifteen minutes later, come out on the right. By giving free rein to my imagination, I felt like an air traffic controller in front of his radar screen.

My concentration was so poor that I could clearly hear the sounds around me. In the kitchen, the cat jumped down from the sink, padded through my bedroom, and tore down the fire escape and into the garden; upstairs, the radio was playing songs by Gainsbourg, and as the volume was higher than usual, I wonder if Kim had invited the girl to her place.

The sound of the radio made me think of a joke I'd heard the week before, on a private radio station.

"Ah!" said the humorist, seeing me smile, "I was beginning to wonder if you'd gone to sleep . . ."

The joke was very short, one brief phrase: "In the winter we often say, 'Shut the door, it's cold outside!' but after the door is shut, it's still just as cold outside." I started to tell it while he looked at me, frowning, and I realized it wasn't going to work. I stopped in mid-sentence.

"I . . . I forget the exact words," I stammered.

That was the only excuse I could come up with. Rolling his eyes, he said with resignation: "I see. Do you think the 'exact words' will come back to you?"

"No," I said.

"Have you got another joke in mind?"

"Not right now."

"If you give it two or three days, do you think you could come up with a humorous situation?"

"No, I don't."

After this series of negative responses, the humorist brought his visit to an end without looking at me, as if we didn't know one another, leaving me alone with the depressing thought that one day, my life would be something uniformly grey and joyless, I who despite my age felt still close to a childhood spent in the light, the bright light of the sun.

20

The Fourth Visit

On my way out of Richard's grocery store one rainy afternoon, I spotted the Old Man at the corner of Des Jardins and Saint-Louis. The rain had made his hat cave in and his resemblance to John Wayne was no more than a distant memory.

He was hesitating over which direction to go. Pretending to read the menu of the Café de la Paix, I kept an eye on him. When I saw him cross rue Saint-Louis and start up the Haldimand hill, I had a hunch that he was on his way to my place. Nothing justified my thinking so, only the fact that he'd come to see me several times before at this late hour, but as a precaution I went home as quickly as I could along the opposite side, taking Saint-Louis and Sainte-Ursule.

At the apartment, I first set down my bag of groceries in the kitchen and put the milk, butter, and chicken in the fridge.

Through the window I saw that I'd guessed right, the Old Man was indeed coming to my place. Though the collar of his raincoat was pulled up and his hat was down over his eyes, I'd have sworn that he was looking up at the window and could see me through the sheer curtain, and I stepped back in spite of myself.

I was upset and irritated.

Why was the Old Man coming so late? Did he think I was completely at his service? And why did he always look so mysterious? Was he playing some little game? Did the Watchman and young Macha have a role in his plans?

While I was turning over these questions in my mind, I heard the three usual sounds of the gate, the stairs, and the waiting room, but I pretended not to. I opened the bottle of Muscat I'd just bought and poured myself half a glass. The Old Man could wait a few minutes, that would show him I had other things to do. I sipped my wine and tried to recall what had happened during his last visit. As it had been recent, I didn't need the computer to bring back the main points. In fact there were only two to keep in mind: the Old Man had forgotten to bring the photo of his wife; he hadn't had a reply to his letter, and I'd written him another one that was rather casual and used a quotation from Chekhov.

My determination to make the Old Man wait crumbled away a minute later. I felt guilty and I wanted to know if my work had finally produced some results, so I opened the door to the waiting room.

"Well, well! Look who's here!" I exclaimed, feigning surprise.

The Old Man didn't reply, but his aggrieved look told me clearly that he wasn't taken in by my words. As soon as he was inside my office, he explained:

"I got an answer from my wife. That's why I'm here so late. I came as soon as I got the letter."

"But . . ." I said, "the mail is delivered in the morning . . ."

"Yes, but I worked all day today."

"In the rain . . ."

"The rain doesn't matter: I put up the hood of the calèche. Some tourists like riding around in the rain. I lend them slickers and rain hats . . ."

"And you?"

"Rain doesn't bother me. Or my horse."

He had an answer to everything. I observed him closely, trying to see what was on his mind, but his chapped and wrinkled face was an impenetrable mask. The strange light that I'd seen in his eyes at certain times now seemed extinguished forever.

I suggested he take off his raincoat and hat, which were dripping onto the floor. Then, holding out my hand, I asked: "Can I have a look at the letter?"

"No," he said.

"Why not?"

"I didn't bring it."

I was so surprised I was speechless. All the efforts we'd made together since spring were aimed at obtaining that letter; I couldn't believe that he'd forgotten it.

"It doesn't matter," he said. "I've read it ten times at least and I know it by heart."

It was pointless to try to make him understand that to me details such as the kind of writing, the size of the paper, the punctuation — even the margins and white spaces — were important. The best thing I could do was help him not forget anything that was in the letter. I asked him a series of questions and he answered them in bits and pieces. His wife said that she was in good health; she was living in the country, along a small river, and she had a garden, flowers, a dog, and a cat; she was glad to hear from him and intended to come and see him soon.

"Oh yes? She said that?"

The Old Man nodded. Strangely enough, he didn't seem altogether glad about what was happening. In his voice I could sense concern, but I didn't pay much attention to it at the time, busy as I was assessing this result, which was more than I could have hoped for.

"She really said she was coming?" I insisted.

"Yes, but she added that for the time being she couldn't tell me the day or the time."

These last words suddenly hit me like a fist in the stomach.

"*The day or the time*: those were her exact words?"

"That's right."

"And how was it signed?"

"Umm . . . it was signed, 'Your wife.'"

"I see. And before the signature, was there some special little remark?"

He scratched his head.

"A little remark?" he repeated.

"Yes, a few words like, 'All my love' or, 'Forever yours' . . ."

"Oh, right!" he said as if he'd suddenly come back to earth. "She wrote, 'See you soon, I hope.'"

"That's not terribly warm, but at least we got the results we wanted, didn't we?"

"Yes."

He stood up, took a few steps, and stopped briefly at the window to look at the sky. The rain had stopped. A little wind must have come up because you could see the leaves stir on the Japanese cherry tree.

"Are you worried about something?" I asked.

"No," he said. "Why?"

"You don't look very happy . . ."

"I'm old," he said simply.

His voice sounded weary, drawling slightly. He came back to sit at my table, crossed his thin legs and, as usual, stuck his hat on his knee.

"What do we do now?" he asked.

"Write another letter. Since she's in a good mood we're going to repeat your invitation, assure her that you'll give her a warm welcome, and try to make her tell you when she intends to come. Does that sound right?"

"Yes."

I opened the drawer and took out my writing implements.

"Shall we start with, 'My love'?" I asked.

"All right."

"Is it a word you were in the habit of using?"

"Yes."

"Very well. But . . . I just remembered. Have you got the photo?"

"What photo?"

"The photo of your wife! Did you bring it?"

"No."

Unable to contain my indignation, I protested sharply.

"That's twice I've asked you for it! Don't tell me you've forgotten it again!"

He gave me a dejected look, then he took his raincoat and hat, and headed for the door without a word. Then he stopped, his hand on the doorknob.

"Last time, you asked me what my wife looked like. I gave you a detailed description. So I thought you wouldn't need a photo now."

With his fingers gripping the doorknob, he waited for my reaction. I could see that he was putting his fate back in my hands. It was up to me to decide: if I agreed that he was right, he would come back and sit down and we'd write the letter to his wife; if I did not agree or even if I said nothing, he would walk out of my office and maybe out of my life as well, and that would be that.

And then I sensed, more clearly than the other times, that some mysterious and powerful ties connected me to this peculiar old man. Ties that were different from a professional relationship. Ties that had something to do with my dead parents, with the drifting soul of my brother, and the uncertain country towards which all of us have been swept along since the world began.

"So," I said, as lightly as possible, "are we going to write that letter?"

To my great relief he let go of the doorknob and came back and sat down. He seemed tired so I just gave him a general outline of the letter and suggested that he leave the details to me; he could come back for it later, whenever it suited him.

He agreed. I was especially glad because I hadn't yet come up with a literary quotation that I could quietly slip into the letter to give it a magical effect; I'd have to do a fair amount of searching in my notebooks and my computer. Before I let him go, I persuaded him to tell me exactly when he intended to come back, and just to be sure, I gave him a card with the date and time for that appointment.

Two days later, when it was time for his visit, the letter was ready. I was pleased with my work. By separating it into three parts — the better to disguise it — I'd found a way to include these words that the journalist Arthur Buies had written to his wife, Mila, which translated fairly well, it seemed to me, the feelings of my client:

My dear wife, be assured that I love you with all my soul, absolutely, entirely, and that the idea which I cherish above all others is to make you happy, and for that reason, to be the best and most affectionate of husbands.

The Old Man didn't come. I listened closely for the three sounds that would announce a visit, but in vain. A quarter of an hour passed, then half a hour, and then I understood that he wasn't going to come.

21

The Aircraft Carrier

By mid-August the days were growing shorter but it was still hot and humid.

I had less work at the office so I took to walking around the neighbourhood. To all appearances I wasn't doing anything in particular, just hanging out, stopping now and then to look at some sight, but actually I was thinking all the time — thinking about the Old Man. He hadn't come to pick up his letter, there hadn't been any sign of him, and I hadn't seen him again in town.

On the Terrasse Dufferin, late in the afternoon, I often stopped to listen to a group of Peruvian musicians who sang folksongs to the accompaniment of a guitar, a drum and an Andean flute. I liked their laid-back manner, their long black hair, their swarthy skin that was more attractive than mine, and I spent a lot of time in their company. Their rhythmical music stirred things that were buried deep inside me, while my idiotic body just stood there, motionless except for the occasional tapping of my foot or nodding of my head. One day another observer showed me what I'd have been able to do if I were normal. As he made his way through the semicircle of spectators in front of the musicians, he began to dance; he followed the rhythm of the music very well while his feet kept inventing new steps and one after the other he raised his bent arms above his head as he spun around. His entire body was in movement and he made me think of a big bird executing a dance of love.

When the music stopped, the dancer was lost in the crowd. I headed for the statue of Champlain, with the idea of strolling through Vieux-Québec wherever I felt like going. All sorts of details caught my eye: the play of light on the river, a tree that was older than me, a cat sleeping on a windowsill, a girl with an enormous backpack, a new book in a store window, the red or blue of a roof . . . But what I was looking for was the Old Man and I didn't see any trace of him. Thought the tourist season wasn't over, his calèche was nowhere to be found.

Finally, I resigned myself to asking the Watchman about him. As much as possible I avoided calling on his services, because he always asked for money, but this time I didn't have a choice: no one was better informed, except maybe Marie, and she was on vacation.

The Watchman wasn't in the minivan or Kim's Range Rover. I found him on the big slope of the Citadelle. He was at the very top, lying on a bench from which he could admire the two arms of the St. Lawrence in the mauve light of the setting sun, with the Île d'Orléans and, at an angle, the receding line of the mountains.

As I came closer I saw that his eyes were closed. A bottle of wine was wedged between his knees. I touched his arm, expecting that he'd repeat the "Indians" gag, but he merely scowled to show that I was disturbing him.

"I wasn't asleep," he said. "I saw you coming. You looked as if your nerves were all on edge."

"I'm sorry," I said.

He held out his bottle.

"Have a slug, it calms the nerves!"

"No, thanks."

"I insist!"

His voice was rather aggressive. To have peace, I took the bottle, wiped its mouth with the tail of my T-shirt, and took a fairly long swig despite the fact that my stomach doesn't tolerate wine between meals very well.

"Well?" he asked.

"It's good stuff!" I declared. Actually that was a blatant lie: it was poor quality, revolting plonk, probably from Ontario. The Watchman took a swig in turn and invited me to sit down.

"Would you take a look at that!" he said, using the neck of the bottle to trace a semicircle that took in the panorama from the Château to the Pointe de Lauzon. "Isn't that the most beautiful landscape in the world?"

I was inclined to agree with him, especially now when a pale bluish mist made it look as if the small sailboats were floating in the air, but because I'm always irritated by people who extoll their native land, I protested at first: "Let's say *one of* the most beautiful!"

"What other place comes to mind?" he asked.

"San Francisco. When you're on a hill and looking at the bay, with the two bridges, the ships, Alcatraz, and the fog banks, it gives pretty much the same impression as here."

"Could be. But still, there's something special here . . ."

"You mean you've got a special way of looking at Quebec?"

"Exactly!"

He was proud of himself and I realized that a skilful manoeuvre on his part had led me to ask that question. Throwing his head back, he took a long swig without offering me any. Which was fine with me.

"Okay. Tell me how you look at it . . ."

"No," he said. "You first."

My way of seeing Quebec City was fairly traditional. I started on an explanation with the hope that a couple of original ideas would come to me along the way. After a few words to evoke the founding of Quebec, the British conquest, and the resistance to assimilation, I added: "In ads about Quebec they often use a photo of the Château Frontenac. But the monument that best illustrates the history of the city, of all Quebec in fact, is that one just behind us."

I half turned towards the Citadelle, the front part of which was a few steps behind us: a rotunda surmounted by a cannon whose sinister-looking dark grey silhouette stood at the far end of Cap Diamant.

The Watchman followed my gaze.

"I know where you're going," he said. "You're going to do the Citadelle number — that tired old cliché about 'the bastion of the French language in America!'"

"I acknowledge it's an old cliché but . . ."

"Besides, it doesn't correspond to reality: everybody knows that the Citadelle was built by the English!"

"You're leaving out one small detail," I said.

He was taking a sip that didn't seem to end. His bottle was nearly vertical in the sunlight and all at once I saw the liquid stop flowing.

"What's that?" he asked.

"Long before the arrival of the British," I said, "the French built a number of fortifications, among them a redoubt and a powder-house in this very spot. In fact you can see vestiges of the powder-house when you visit the Citadelle."

Tucking the nearly empty bottle between his knees, he gave an admiring whistle; I couldn't tell if it was motivated by my knowledge of history or by his appreciation of cheap red wine. To dispel any ambiguity I wanted to conclude with a striking turn of phrase.

"The city of Quebec has been and is still the bastion of French in America!"

"I don't see it like that," he said. "When I've had a fair amount to drink, I mean a few bottles, there's a special thing that happens — providing I don't fall asleep . . ."

"What's that?" I asked, because it seemed very clear that he was waiting for the question before he went on. This time, he held the bottle out to me but I pushed it away gently.

"It happens when I'm lying on my back," he went on, getting up to stretch out on the grass. "It's as if part of my body comes away and goes up into the air . . . Has that ever happened to you?"

"It's probably your 'astral body,'" I said ironically, remembering something I'd read in one of Kim's books.

"It is? . . . Well, anyway, I feel as if I'm very high in the air, floating above the river, and it changes the way I see the city. Terrasse Dufferin and the Château look like a big aircraft-carrier that's about to cast off and set sail on all the seas in the world . . ."

His alcoholic's red eyes stared into the mist. As he spoke he waved his arms in a way that embraced the horizon, and it was all of Quebec that I saw break away from the shore and go out to sea to "join its voice to the concert of the nations," as they wrote in the history textbooks of the past.

Lying beside him with my eyes half closed, I let myself be overcome by images of a Quebec sailing freely in international waters. Suddenly, the sound of snoring put an end to my reverie. The Watchman had gone to sleep, totally smashed once again, and that was when I remembered why I was here: I'd come to ask if he'd heard anything about the Old Man. Alas! It was too late; he was in no condition to give me an answer.

22

The Young
Writer's Dream

As I didn't find the Old Man on the esplanade of rue d'Auteuil or on Place d'Armes or in the places where young Macha could sometimes be seen, I was getting seriously worried. I was reduced to wondering if the impatience I'd shown during his last visit was the reason for his disappearance.

One afternoon I decided to check and see if he was still living on 26th Street in Limoilou. Taking the manuscript of a novel a publisher had asked me to assess, and a bag of cookies, I drove the minivan down to the Lower Town. As I'd done in the spring, when he and I had, so to speak, shared the emotions of a hockey game, I parked on the street that ran perpendicular to his building. As long as I didn't attract attention, it was the best place from which to keep an eye on his third-floor apartment without rousing the suspicion of the neighbours.

In the Volks, I drew the curtain on the rear window all the way and those on the side windows partway, then I opened up the table and started to read the manuscript. I just had to raise my head and I could see the apartment or the entrance to the building.

The manuscript had a blue cover on which you could see a Yamaha 500 racing model crouching and ready to leap. It was the first novel by a very young man and I realized right away that he had talent. The story got off to a quick start, it moved along briskly, and you wanted to skip some sections to find out what was going to happen. I did my best not to read too quickly, stopping now and then to look at the building.

Half an hour later, when I took a break for coffee and cookies, I was already favourably disposed towards the author. For the fun of it, I imagined being his publisher and pulling out all the stops in what I fantasized as "the young writer's dream." For instance, he would phone me to ask about his manuscript and I'd invite him to come and see me the next morning. He'd turn up at my office first thing, worried and intimidated, and I'd start by telling him that, unfortunately, I hadn't had time to read his manuscript. Then I would ask him to sit down. On the wall facing him would hang a poster with the following dreadful remark by the American journalist H.L. Mencken in big print: "Many are the writers who have ruined their careers by publishing too soon." Then I would open the young author's blue book, pretending I was seeing what was written there for the first time. And then I'd start to read. I would read the whole story in one go, as if I were carried away by the narrative, without once looking up at my visitor. When I got to the words "The End," I would look at my watch, like someone coming back from far away, and make as if I were leaving my office when the young man would clear his throat to remind me that he was there. I would say: "What the hell are you doing here?" He would reply timidly: "I'm the author . . ." And then I would say the words that every young writer dreams of hearing: "You are? . . . Well! This is the most wonderful story I've ever read!"

I enjoyed imagining the author's surprised and delighted expression, but it didn't mean that I forgot to see if anything was going on in the Old Man's apartment. The curtains on the third floor were wide open and I couldn't see anyone at the window. The screaming siren of an ambulance, probably speeding towards St. Francis of Assisi Hospital, ripped through the air down the length of 26th Street, bringing people to their windows or onto their balconies and piercing my heart, but there was nothing going on in the Old Man's apartment.

My coffee finished, I decided to see if his name was still on the mailbox. I went inside without a sound and saw his name there: Sam Miller. I went to the end of the corridor and, glancing through the window in the door that opened onto the back, I noticed that the Ford pickup wasn't there. I went up to the third floor then and rang at his apartment. A two-note bell chimed and I resisted the urge to make a run for it. There was no answer. I rang again: still nothing.

I went back down the stairs and in spite of my shyness, I rang at the second-floor apartment. The door opened a crack on a pot-bellied man in a flowered shirt.

"What do you want?" he snarled.

"Sorry to bother you," I said. "There's no answer from the old gentleman who lives upstairs and . . ."

"And what? He doesn't have to answer!"

"You're quite right, but I'm worried because I haven't seen him for a few days now. And the curtains are open and you can't see anyone . . ."

"Are you related?"

"Yes."

It wasn't an out-and-out lie because answering in the affirmative I'd thought, "spiritually related," which constituted a mental restriction. But I was very surprised to hear myself add: "He's my father."

The fat man opened the door all the way. He looked me up and down and searched my face, no doubt searching for signs of the kinship I'd just claimed.

"If you can't see him at the living-room window," he explained less harshly, "the reason's very simple: he'd rather stay in the kitchen. He's allowed to do that, isn't he?"

"Of course he is," I said. "I hadn't thought of that . . . But tell me, do you hear him walking around now and then?"

A little woman with frizzy hair came up behind the man as I asked that question.

"Oh, yes," she said, "we can hear him when we're in the kitchen too."

"Just now, though, we don't hear him very much," said the man.

"Maybe he wears slippers . . ."

"I haven't seen him go in or out for a few days now."

"And his old Ford isn't in the parking lot . . ."

They went on talking to each other as if I weren't there, then the little woman turned to me.

"If you're his son, why don't we see more of you?"

The question was relevant. I couldn't think of a reply and for want of anything better, I bowed my head and tried to look guilty. Just as the man was closing the door again, I had the presence of mind to ask: "Could you tell me if he has any visitors? Say, a very young girl with dark skin, eyes as black as coal, and a wild look about her?"

They regarded one another.

"Yes," said the woman, "she's been here a couple of times. She'll come at night and go in through the back door."

"One morning I saw her at the mailbox," said the man. "She'd opened the old fellow's box. All at once she turned around and I thought she was going to jump on me and scratch. She looked like a wild cat . . . Have you ever run into one when you were walking in the woods? A real one, I mean, what people call a 'bobcat'?"

"Yes," I said, "it happened to me once."

An image came back to me, all dried up and broken into pieces. I tried for a moment to stick them together, and when I opened my eyes again the big man had shut his door. I went back to the Volks. As I was driving down 1st Avenue on my way home, the image became clear by itself.

The wild cat, looking haughty and fierce, was sitting on a log that was part of a dam that beavers had built at the outlet of a lake. It was the lake where my father used to take us trout-fishing when we were little. Some days, if there weren't many customers in the store, or simply because he wanted a break, he would ask if by any chance one of us might feel like going to the cottage. There was pandemonium: we would put on our oldest pants, dig some worms, fix a lunch based on cookies and peanut butter sandwiches, and pile into the pickup truck that would be willing to start half the time.

That day the fishing wasn't good; we had cast our lines in vain at all the places where luck had smiled on us in the past. Then my father weighed anchor, letting the rowboat drift along with the breeze that heralded rain and that finally sent us towards the sea-wall. Suddenly, ten metres from shore, my father spotted the wild cat. He quickly put the anchor back in the water. He pointed to the animal and, with the same gesture, told us not to move. In any event, surprise kept me from making the slightest movement. With his round head, tufts of white fur in the ears, and reddish-brown, lightly spotted fur, the big cat looked threatening and I was sure that with one heave he could pounce on us in the rowboat. But after a moment that seemed very long to me, he got up, turned around, and made his way slowly and nonchalantly towards the edge of the woods.

꒜

All the spaces on Saint-Denis were taken so I parked the minivan on Sainte-Ursule, thinking that I'd move it the first chance I got so as not to complicate life for the Watchman. On my way into the garden, I saw young Macha, sitting on the grass with her back against the Japanese cherry tree. Her knees were pulled up with a book on them, and Pretty Cat was curled in a ball at her feet. The brown skin of her knees and her thighs showed through some rips in her jeans. When I said hello, she responded with a nod, not looking up, but I couldn't be annoyed: for her, every book seemed to be a kind of castle where you could walk as you pleased, shut out the real world, even get lost in its dungeons.

After I'd showered and exchanged my jeans for shorts and my shoes for sandals, I decided to go up to Kim's place. I knocked gently on her door; she opened it and asked me to follow her into the kitchen where she was cooking supper. The first thing I saw, in spite of her apron, was that she was wearing her most beautiful kimono, the blue silk one with the big green Solomon Islands butterfly on the back.

"Did you have a good day?" she asked.

"Not particularly," I said. "What are you making?"

"Scalloped potatoes."

She was holding a vegetable knife, so instead of putting her arms around my neck as she usually did, she kissed my cheeks, keeping her hands behind her back, Then she pressed her whole body against mine; the softness of her breasts against my chest was a consolation after the bad luck that had followed me for a good part of the day.

I felt a very powerful urge to caress her and merge with her in a shared warmth. I untied her apron but stopped almost at once, afraid of being like one of those ridiculous characters in the movies who flings a woman onto the kitchen table in the midst of the dishes and cutlery, and grabs the tablecloth, sending all the dishes to the floor at the moment of what Kim and I call ironically "the seismic tremor."

Kim smiled and the light I could see in her eyes was so warm and inviting that, thinking she was encouraging me, I began to caress her back and, stealthily, the top of her buttocks, and to kiss her neck and the edge of her ear. She pushed me away very gently, then she crouched in front of the stove, switched on the oven light, and looked in at her scalloped potatoes.

"Nearly ready," she said.

"It smells delicious," I said.

"Did you see young Macha when you got here?"

"Yes."

"I invited her to eat with us, but she didn't say yes or no; she just smiled."

"She did?"

I was surprised and a little jealous; I couldn't remember seeing her smile before.

"Would you go to the window and let her know that she can come up?" asked Kim.

"Sure."

On my way through her bedroom to the fire escape, I couldn't help looking — this time apprehensively — at the oval mirror on the dressing table that was surrounded by old postcards and photos, and I lingered for a moment on the three photos of Kim with a little girl.

When I got to the landing, it was Pretty Cat who noticed me first. It took her a fraction of a second to realize that this was about food and, abandoning the girl, she trotted up the metal steps and raced into the bedroom through the French window.

I whistled softly and Macha looked up.

"Supper's ready," I articulated in a very low voice as I mimed putting something in my mouth; I didn't want to speak up because of the people walking by on the street.

Instead of replying, she became engrossed in her book again. I feigned nonchalance, but as soon as I was back inside I glanced out the French window and saw that she was on her way. She climbed the steps slowly, still absorbed in her book.

Inside the apartment she didn't say hello to either of us, but sat in a corner with her book and waited to be served. She didn't let go of it all through the meal, holding it in her left hand, next to her plate, and she barely took her eyes off it whenever she took a mouthful of potatoes. It was *The Eye of the Wolf*, a novel by Daniel Pennac.

She only consented to close her book at dessert, when she saw that it was a butterscotch sundae. Kim asked her what the novel was about. The girl came alive then, her black eyes glimmered in a way that lit up her obstinate features, and she said that it was about an Alaskan wolf that lived in a cage in a zoo and was called "the blue wolf." He just had one eye, having lost the other one when the men had captured him, and since that time he hated and despised all human beings.

The girl pushed her chair back and got up, pacing the kitchen to show how contemptuously the wolf paced in his cage. She walked without making the slightest sound, barefoot on the tiles, her shoulders hunched, hair falling over one eye, body seemingly charged with electricity. That girl was the very image of life, and as I glanced at Kim I could see that she was as fascinated as I was.

23

A Weekend at
Bottomless Lake

The following Friday, Kim decided to spend the weekend at Bottomless Lake with young Macha. I was not invited, but I wouldn't have gone anyway, because I still hadn't found the Old Man. We had agreed that Pretty Cat, who was very attached to her tree and to her territory, would stay with me. But just as they were about to leave she jumped inside the Range Rover and settled on the knees of the girl, who had turned her jeans into cut-offs.

I went back inside and I don't know why but I locked the door on the main floor, which we usually kept open for the homeless. Because of the strange kind of heart that I had, Kim didn't always represent the same thing to me. Depending on the day, she was my girlfriend, my mother, or my sister, and sometimes, when my emotions clouded over like troubled waters, she became a person of my sex.

That day, she represented my mother, which was why I took my troubled soul through the three rooms of the apartment. In the end I positioned myself at the kitchen window to observe the passersby, and gradually the image of the Range Rover and its occupants was erased from my mind, slipping towards that unknown place where dreams, regrets, and illusions go as well.

The Old Man's disappearance still worried me but I didn't know where to look for him. Even the Watchman, who generally knew about the comings and goings of everyone in Vieux-Québec, didn't know what had happened to him. All that I'd learned from my investigation was that his horse and calèche were in a stable at the Parc des Expositions as usual, and that he'd left money to feed his horse for a few days.

His absence now, in late August, was all the more surprising because the city was overrun with Japanese tourists who were wealthier than other visitors and very enthusiastic about the exotic. From my window I could see a small group of them: they were at the corner of rue Sainte-Ursule, looking lost and studying a map of the neighbourhood. From their motions they seemed to be hesitating between the Château and the Citadelle.

While I kept watching the passersby I was trying to think of a way to find the Old Man, hoping for some new idea. I was wasting my time; ideas never came when I made an effort, they came when I least expected them. That day then I decided to go out, and because it was cooler, I was hesitating between a sweatshirt and a real sweater when it occurred to me that old Marie might be back from her vacation. I phoned the Relais at once and it was she who answered.

I hurried over to see her. She poured me a coffee and when I asked, without really expecting much, if she'd heard anything about the Old Man, she nodded. She hadn't seen him herself but one of the calèche drivers had spotted him in the middle of the afternoon on the Terrasse Dufferin; he hadn't been working, he was leaning on the guardrail near the funicular and looking out at the river. I told Marie that her freckles were very seductive, then I drained my cup in one gulp to conceal my embarrassment and rushed to the Terrasse.

The Old Man wasn't there beside the funicular. The chance that he would still be there was nil, but I'd been hoping that he would be, though common sense suggested otherwise. I started walking slowly then, looking at everyone, intending to explore the entire length of the promenade. As well as the musicians from Peru, there were jugglers, clowns, a one-man band and a couple of old American crooners. I'd known all these buskers for ages, but suddenly, opposite the ice cream stand, I was across from a violinist I was seeing for the first time.

She was in the very middle of the promenade, her violin case at her feet, and people who had just noticed her took a detour behind her. Wearing a long dress and delicate flat-heeled shoes, she was playing classical music, her eyes half closed, her head swaying with restraint and a kind of discretion.

Seeing that everyone else was detouring around her, I stopped to listen. I was facing her at an angle ten paces away. She was playing a rather austere piece that I thought might be a Bach sonata. The chin rest of her violin had been replaced by a bit of black velvet, because of its softness no doubt. No sooner had I noticed it than the piece was over. Since I was the only listener I wasn't too sure what to do. Maybe I should have dropped a dollar into her case, murmured *au revoir* and continued on my way, but I'd just got there and I'd only heard the last few bars.

The violinist turned her head in my direction, smiled shyly and started playing again; I thought it might be Mozart, but I wasn't too sure. She didn't look much older than twenty; she was probably a student who needed money. The strollers continued to step behind her to avoid her. I could hear flaws in her playing, but when I realized that she was playing just for me and that she was putting all her soul into it, tears came to my eyes. If I really thought about it, it was an emotion so keen that it couldn't be only on account of the music: there was surely another reason, but just then I didn't know what it was.

My emotion dispersed, I rummaged discreetly in the pocket of my jeans in search of a loonie or four quarters. I'd intended to continue on my way as soon as she'd finished playing and I had thanked her tangibly. But after she stopped and just as I was about to carry out my plan, she suddenly turned towards me and, smiling very gently, bowed to express her delight at having had a listener. No doubt she thought that I'd also earned a little break, because she launched into a new piece right away. It was a jig, Vigneault's "Danse à Saint-Dilon," and as if by magic the passersby stopped. In no time she had an impressive semicircle of very interested listeners, among them a group of Japanese tourists, and I took advantage of the situation to slip away, after dropping a dollar into her violin case.

I went to the end of the Terrasse but didn't spot the Old Man. On my way back, seeing that there were only two or three people in front of the violinist, I chickened out and, like the others, slipped behind her. Then I took the stairs next to the Château and went home along rue Mont-Carmel. Patches of fog clung to the slope of the Citadelle and night was falling more quickly than it had on previous days.

I made myself a chicken sandwich and ate it without much appetite, sitting on the sill of the French door that opened onto the garden, where the grey shapes of Pretty Cat's friends were prowling.

As it wasn't fully dark yet, I could see that the leaves on the vine above the Cats' Tree were now bright red. I tossed some scraps of chicken to the cats, then went inside.

After wandering for a long time through the empty house, going up and down the stairs, I went into my office. I was pacing the room as usual when I noticed, pinned to the wall under the photo of the Crouching Scribe, a bit of paper on which I recognized Kim's handwriting. I went to look at it. It was an invitation to go up to her place: there was something special for me in her bedroom.

Intrigued but a little anxious, too, I climbed the stairs and pushed open her bedroom door. Groping my way in the dim light, I switched on the lamp at the head of the bed and discovered on the bedside table a book that I didn't know. I drew the curtains to protect myself from the neighbours across the way, then I examined the book. It was *The Old Man Who Read Love Stories*, by Luis Sepulveda. Inside it, a note from Kim on blue paper read: "I'm leaving you this book to help you pass the time; it reminds me of the old man you're looking for. I love you. Kim."

I took the book into her office, which was a compromise between a psychologist's office and a physiotherapy room. I particularly liked the multiple-position treatment table, and the tatami and the big rocking chair, but what caught my attention most was the relaxation chair.

There was nothing more comfortable to read in than this chair and I sat in it whenever I could. It resembled the long padded chairs used in blood donation centres. When you sat in it, your back was at an angle, your knees raised, your arms supported by wide armrests: it was the ideal position for those like me who were afflicted with back pain. And then, there was a somewhat unsettled atmosphere in, made up of little nothings and things invented that got tangled up for my greater pleasure: the fragrance of lemon-scented ointments, the furtive gliding of hands on skin, murmurs and confidences, maybe even sweet words and caresses.

I got comfortable in my chair and started to read, and before long the author's "little music" produced its effect: from the very first page, I felt close to the old man in the title, whose name was Antonio José Bolivar Proano, no less. He lived by himself in a bamboo hut on the shore of the Nangaritza River in Peru. Like me, he had a back problem that kept him from sitting for long periods. And so he stood to read his love stories, leaning on a tall table specially built for eating and reading, facing a window that looked out on the river. I had a good laugh at one of his quirks: he had a denture that had cost a pretty penny and to keep from wearing it out unnecessarily, he would remove it and keep it in his pocket, carefully wrapped in his handkerchief.

An expert on the Amazonian forest, the old man was put in charge of following a cat — most likely an ocelot — that was suspected of killing a man. He went deep into the forest and I followed the cat's trail with him for a while — and then to my shame I fell asleep in my overly comfortable chair. I had a dream that was filled with wild cats, one-eyed wolves, and bloodthirsty ocelots.

When I woke up it was time for bed, but of course I wasn't sleepy. Looking out the window, I saw that the fog was thicker — a sign that autumn was coming. I decided to go out for a walk in the neighbourhood.

24

A Fog that
Rose off the River

In all my life I don't remember seeing such dense fog. It came off the river and crept into the area inside the walls, making everything look ghostly and unreal.

As I was crossing rue Saint-Louis, the bell of the Notre-Dame-du-Sacré-Coeur church marked two A.M. Farther away, at the corner of rue Sainte-Anne, just as I was wondering whether to go towards rue Saint-Jean or the river, which attracted me as always, I heard a calèche. I thought I recognized the slight limp of the Old Man's horse. I jumped back and hid in the entrance of a building. My imagination had played a trick on me, because when the calèche went past, swallowed up at once by the fog, its lantern swaying in the rear, I had enough time to see that the person holding the reins was not the Old Man.

This incident made me want to check again to see if the Old

Man's calèche was on Place d'Armes. When I got there I noticed two calèches parked behind one another on the street going up to the Château. I went closer and saw that one was the Old Man's; I recognized his dapple-grey horse, but he himself wasn't there.

"Feel like going for a ride?"

It was the driver of the second calèche. He was sitting on the front seat with a blanket around his shoulders. His quiet, jaunty voice rose up like music in the fog and he had long hair tied at the nape of his neck so that I wasn't actually sure if it was a man or a woman. I pointed to the calèche without a driver.

"No, thanks, I just wanted to have a word with the Old Man."

"Monsieur Miller?" asked the gentle voice. "He's away."

"I can see that, but he can't be very far if his calèche is here . . ."

"Are you with the police?"

"What? . . . No, no, absolutely not!"

I protested vigorously but to tell the truth, I was relieved to see that the people around the Old Man tried to protect him. And most of all, I was delighted that I'd finally found his trace.

"He went for a walk," said the gentle voice.

"Which way?"

"That way."

A gloved hand emerged from under the blanket and pointed to the post office to the left of Terrasse Dufferin.

"Thanks," I said.

"We thought that with this fog, lovers would be in the mood for a calèche ride. Fog is romantic . . . You can earn as much in one night as in a whole week, but it has to be a light mist, the kind that frays . . . Tonight it's too thick; people can't see anything and they're afraid. We guessed wrong. There were three of us calèches and one has already left."

"Thanks a lot," I said. "And good luck for the rest of the night."

"If you see Monsieur Miller, tell him I'll be leaving soon."

Nodding, I made a vague farewell gesture that could be intended for either a woman or a man, then I made my way to the post office.

The closer you got to the river, the thicker the fog. The yellow and green lights that usually created an illuminated crown on the main tower of the Château had disappeared and the few windows that were lit up seemed to be suspended in space. I could make out the dark silhouette of the Champlain monument and in the back, the first streetlamps on the Terrasse.

Turning my back on the founder of Quebec, I started down rue du Fort, glancing into every corner, including the steps of the various staircases that surrounded the secondary entrance to the post office and the statue of Monseigneur de Laval. Every ten paces I detoured to inspect one of the places where the habitués of Vieux-Québec hung out, then I went back on the road. I could hardly see a thing and the dampness was seeping right into my bones.

At the top of the Côte de la Montagne, I decided not to start down right away. It seemed more logical to inspect first Parc Montmorency and the beginning of rue des Remparts. I entered the little park, trying not to walk on the dead leaves and branches. I intended simply to make a semicircle and then get back onto rue des Remparts, across from the Grand Séminaire. Suddenly, I spied the Old Man; he was bending over the stone parapet that looked out over the cliff, in the corner closest to the Côte de la Montagne. In spite of the fog, his long silhouette and his hat were easy to recognize.

I stood there, glued to the spot, wondering anxiously what he was doing there, bent forward with his hands on the parapet. He straightened up and lit a cigarette; the flame of his lighter cast a yellow glow in the mist. Assuming that he was going to turn around and leave the park, I hid behind the base of the statue of George

Étienne Cartier. A few seconds later, he walked past the statue and disappeared onto a small staircase leading to the left-hand sidewalk on the Côte de la Montagne. I let the sound of his footsteps die away, then I set out after him.

It was impossible to see him on the hill because the fog was even thicker. I could, however, hear the sound of his heavy shoes. And because I had on tennis shoes, he couldn't hear me.

Just before the spot where the hill turns left, I stopped to listen. The footsteps had a different sound, which meant that the Old Man had taken the big staircase whose three flights went down to the small streets in the Lower Town. I ran down the first two flights, then took the third more slowly. At the bottom of the stairs, most likely because we were level with the river, the fog was no longer a solid mass: it glided along at ground level in scattered patches. On rue Sous-le-Fort, the damp paving stones shone intermittently in the light of the streetlamps.

Footsteps on the left drew my attention. Between two banks of fog I could make out the Old Man's hunched silhouette turning the corner of the lane that ended up at Notre-Dame-des-Victoires church. I had no way of knowing if he'd noticed me or not. I walked on tiptoe to that intersection and when he crossed Place Royale at an angle, I let him get a little ahead of me. I didn't know what he had in mind, but I was glad I hadn't lost him in the night. I waited a few moments before I resumed my shadowing. Completely deserted now, Place Royale seemed like a film set; the fog gave a mysterious look to the house fronts and the monuments, and some scenes from *The Third Man*, accompanied by the well-known zither music, filed past in my head.

Now I left Place Royale. I spotted the Old Man at the end of a lane that went directly to the river; he had only to cross rue Dalhousie. He was about to do so when a taxi going too fast in the fog nearly knocked him down. I saw him then heading for the first intersection; he waited for the light to turn green, then he crossed the street and started pacing the Pointe-à-Carcy wharf.

A little breeze that had come up on the river was beginning to disperse the fog and I risked being spotted. I went to rue Saint-Jacques, where I realized that, if necessary, I could take shelter behind a wall of the Musée de la Civilisation. On the wharf, the Old Man was walking with his head down, hands stuffed in the pockets of his raincoat, hat over his eyes. I was hugging the wall of the building when he came close to me. A sightseeing boat that was fast asleep was berthed across from the pier. My heart sank every time I heard the lowing of the foghorns on ships that were gliding, barely visible, along the water.

All at once the Old Man came to a halt. Turning towards the river, he went to the edge of the wharf and for a moment I stopped breathing. As the fog dissipated I could see him step onto a cement block that served as a buffer and lean over as if to watch the water travelling towards the sea. All at once, a light came on in my head. The idea was so simple, so clear, I wondered why I hadn't thought of it sooner: the Old Man — like me on account of my heart — thought about death a great deal. Death both attracted and frightened him, and it was to her — though he did not yet know it — that the letters he'd asked me to write to his wife were intended. Death was for him an attractive and dangerous woman.

When he finally straightened up and walked away from the edge of the river, I felt tremendously relieved. The fog had lifted almost completely. He went away in the direction of the Upper Town and I could hear the familiar sound of his heavy shoes die away in the cold night.

I didn't follow him.

25

A Rustling of Wings

The first thing that my friend Kim did on Sunday night when she came back from her weekend at Bottomless Lake with Macha and Pretty Cat was to invite me up for a drink.

On the inside staircase, I ran into young Macha who was tearing down the stairs with a book under her arm. When I wished her good evening she couldn't answer because she was wolfing down a big handful of chips. Her face, ordinarily so obstinate, was illuminated by a light similar to the one that can be seen in the eyes of a tame animal. She had on new clothes; in her hooded navy sweatshirt, jeans in Kim's favourite shade of blue, and black Reebok boots, she cut a fine figure.

Kim was in the kitchen. She held out half a glass of well-chilled Muscat, then changed her mind and kissed me on the mouth, tracing the outline of my lips with the tip of my tongue. It was a little unexpected; usually when we got together after an absence she snuggled up to me so I could feel all the warmth of her body.

Somewhat nervously, she rummaged in the fridge and took out a pot; she lifted the lid, then switched on the fluorescent light above the stove to inspect the contents.

"There's pot-au-feu from the other day," she said. "Would you like to eat with us?"

"I'd love to! Is Macha coming back?"

"She said she was, but she didn't say when."

"How was your weekend at the lake?"

"It was fine, but it turned cold. It was as if fall arrived all at once. Instead of going out in the canoe we stayed inside, sitting on the sofa wrapped in blankets, with a fire in the fireplace."

She sipped some Muscat. On her face I thought I could see the same soft light that I'd seen on the girl's, but then she briskly turned her back and went to heat up the stew.

"What about here?"

"Same thing," I said. "In the garden, the whole vine turned red practically overnight."

"Looks like it froze during the night."

"Yes," I said. Then I fell silent, expecting her to ask if I'd heard anything about the Old Man . . . She didn't, though; she seemed to have forgotten that it had been my main concern for weeks now. I couldn't be angry with her, she had her own worries.

Every fall, she got requests for help from all over. With the cold weather, she had to see a number of patients who had a greater need for comfort and for human warmth. For me too, there was no lack of work: besides the usual CVs, I'd undertaken to revise the autobiography of a former singing star and to draw up an English-French lexicon of sports terms.

"You're sure you're all right?" asked Kim.

"Yes," I said, "I was thinking about my work and yours."

"As far as mine's concerned, there's going to be a little change: it won't be easy but I'm going to try to stop working nights."

"Really?"

She nodded and took several sips in a row, watching me over the rim of her glass. I asked: "Because of Macha?"

"Yes," she said. "Are you pleased?"

"Sure."

Maybe she thought I was delighted about Macha's arrival . . . What was actually making me happy was the thought that I wouldn't be wakened in the middle of the night by the metallic vibrations of the fire escape and that I'd no longer feel a secret and shameful jealousy when I saw shadows go past my window on their way upstairs.

"Are you hungry?" she asked.

"A little," I said. "You?"

"Me too." She took the lid off the pot, stirred the contents with a wooden spoon, and tasted the broth.

"It's ready," she said. "Do you want to eat right away?"

"Gladly."

The table was set for three. I brought her the plates and she served us. The dish was still very good. After supper, Macha still hadn't come back. Kim took my hand and led me to her bedroom as she'd done dozens of time before, with that mixture of tenderness and firmness that suited me so well.

On my way into the bedroom, I saw the khaki canvas bag that Macha had brought, with US ARMY inscribed in black; it was hanging by a strap from the doorknob. There was nothing remarkable about it aside from the fact that it held all of young Macha's worldly goods, but when I saw it hanging from the doorknob I couldn't help seeing it as the emblem of a victorious battle. The thought made me laugh and I was still chuckling nervously when Kim started to undress me.

"What are you laughing at?" she asked.

I couldn't reply because it was the kind of thing that seems twice as absurd and ridiculous when you try to explain it. My silence made her look cross; she toppled me onto the bed and started tickling me while she finished taking off my clothes.

"I'm not laughing at anything," I said.

"No? Are you sure?" she asked, tickling my underarms and belly. I was at her mercy. I was stark naked, I was doubled over laughing, I had tears in my eyes, and begged her to stop.

Her tickling went on forever until, realizing that my tears were winning out over my laughter, she began to caress me in a gentle way that reminded me of the first times we'd been together. I started to undress her and at that very moment Macha appeared in the doorway. There hadn't been a sound from the stairs or the kitchen.

She stepped back.

Kim pulled up a sheet to cover us up to the waist.

"Am I in the way?" asked the girl in a barely audible voice.

"No," said Kim.

"Not at all," I said.

That barefaced lie won me a smile from Kim that was like the continuation of our interrupted caresses. She asked the girl: "Do you want something to eat?"

"I'm not hungry," she replied. Her head was down, a lock of curly hair covered one eye, and she was leaning against the doorpost.

Kim drew herself up on one elbow, with a knowing smile that meant, "Sure you aren't." She started to get up but Pretty Cat, who had come inside with the girl, jumped onto the foot of the bed and began to lick her paws and rub them against her muzzle; she'd probably emptied the stew pot and cleaned the plates that we'd left on the table.

Her washing finished, Pretty Cat began to snoop around on the bed, obviously looking for a way to slip under the sheet. Kim lifted it, helped the cat get comfortable in the warmth, and moved to my side to give her more room. Then she held out her hand to Macha.

The girl approached, looking down, and sat on the edge of the bed. She didn't say anything and all we could hear was the purring of Pretty Cat under the sheet and, now and then, the sound of a car on avenue Sainte-Geneviève. After a minute or two, Kim lifted the sheet again and I held my breath while the girl slipped into the bed.

She was just a very young girl, still a child, and I could have almost sworn that I heard a rustling of wings when she slipped under the sheet, but there was something in her that was as hard as a diamond, something pure and uncompromising that made me realize that my time in the rust-coloured brick house was nearing its end.

Kim squarely turned her back to me, then she put her arms around the child and I could see by squinting that they were being very careful not to crush the cat. As I had no clothes on it was hard for me to leave, but after half an hour or so, their regular breathing told me they'd fallen asleep. I got up discreetly. I was unbeatable at getting out of a bed without disturbing anyone.

After I'd picked up my clothes, I went down the inside staircase to my place. Pretty Cat decided to come along and she jumped silently out of the bed. I've always admired the way that cats descend stairs so smoothly, in a single, very graceful movement, as if they were sliding down an icy slope. In my bedroom I opened the French door and went outside with her for a moment, standing naked on the landing. I saw her race down the fire escape, go around the garden, sniffing the odours, then climb up to her usual place on the highest board in the Cats' Tree. The air was abnormally cool for the season, there was a halo around the moon, and when I went inside I remembered that the forecast had told us to expect the first snowfall.

I got dressed very quickly because of the cold. After I'd stuffed a few things in a suitcase, I lay down to rest for a moment. I fell asleep and dreamed that the first snow had fallen.

It was falling onto the garden, onto the Cats' Tree and onto my bed.